MOON OVER THE MEDITERRANEAN

Published by Brolga Publishing Pty Ltd
ABN 46 063 962 443
PO Box 12544
A'Beckett St
Melbourne, VIC, 8006
Australia

email: markzocchi@brolgapublishing.com.au

National Library of Australia
Cataloguing-in-Publication data
    G J Maher, author.
    ISBN 9781925367898 (paperback)
    Subjects: Travel. Travelers' writings, Australian.
    Travel writing.

Cover design by Alice Cannet
Typesetting by Elly Cridland

BE PUBLISHED

Publish through a successful publisher. National Distribution, Dennis Jones & Associates
International Distribution to the United Kingdom, North America.
Sales Representation to South East Asia
Email: markzocchi@brolgapublishing.com.au

MOON OVER THE MEDITERRANEAN

G J Maher

For
Barbara

'You must be the change you wish to see in the world.'

- Mahatma Gandhi.

CHAPTER ONE

L et me tell you a story, one full of learning and intrigue, travels and inspiration. It won't take long. Sit back and relax. Make yourself comfortable. Perhaps you could close your eyes and dream a little as I relate the story of someone I met a long time ago, a dear friend of mine. Imagine an ever so gentle breeze touching gently on your face, the aromas of sage, chamomile, wheat and barley in your nostrils, aromas so prevalent in Greece and her islands. Just sit and think for a moment as you read these words. Imagine the sounds: the chorus of the cicadas, their song reaching your ears in waves, a distant horn from an arriving ship, birds singing in the shade of the sparsely positioned trees. Look at the colours that might catch your attention: the delicate mauve of the chaste tree whose stems have been used for centuries to make wicker items for the home and market; the bright red of the cherry tree loved not only for its tangy fruit but also for its prized wood; the pomegranate, pear, apple, fig and olive and of course the grapes, and a thousand herbs, bright colours and subtle ones too, colours of the entire spectrum amidst the brown, often dried earth of the islands of the Aegean.

The year is 1967 and Alexander was yet to discover any of this. He was on board a small passenger ship, the Portokalis Ilios, on her maiden Greek voyage departing Piraeus and he was bound for Santorini eventually, although he would have to change ships to get there.

It was 9 am and already the sun was hot. It's like that in a Greek summer, always hot, the sky always blue. Alexander had never been to Greece before. He had also never been on a ship, so everything was new. Alexander was born in a little village in the south of Holland. His family had been cobblers for generations. His father and grandfather ran the family business there, but Alexander didn't want any of it. He found shoes boring and couldn't imagine making them and repairing them for the rest of his life. If anything, he'd have preferred to follow in his mother's footsteps as a cook. Her stroopwafels, oliebollen and poffertjes were simply exquisite. Dutch cooking was not known for being the best in Europe, so Alexander's mother, in her patisserie, specialised in German and French sweets and had become so well-known that she supplied other patisseries in a hundred-kilometre radius around her shop. At the end of her fifth year in business, she had eleven staff, and now, ten years later, she had a factory too and employed fifty. But Alexander didn't want this to be his job either.

In fact he didn't know what he wanted to do with his life, apart from travel and see the world. At 19, he could wait no longer, and so here he was after a bus trip from Amsterdam to Athens, leaning on the railing of a ship with the wind in his hair, heading to an island he knew nothing about, Tinos.

Why, you may ask, had Alexander chosen this island? It's quite simple really. When he had reached the port of Piraeus early that morning, after journeying from Amsterdam to Athens, Tinos was the only island with a ferry leaving for it that morning. Remember the year. In 1967 there were far fewer ferries travelling around the Mediterranean than there are today. That changed in the decades that followed, but back then, Alexander's ferry was one of only three leaving on that day, and it was the first.

The month was June and, as I said, it was already hot, in the thirties in fact and not a breath of wind. The Portokalis Ilios was a slow boat and it took all morning to reach the island, but when it did, Alexander was greeted with something that would mark him forever.

Ropes were skilfully tossed ashore by hardened sailors whose facial features and gnarled hands told a thousand stories. Slowly the hydraulics of the ramp kicked into action and Alexander watched from behind a small crowd of locals as they prepared to disembark. Vehicles started up and belched choking smoke over the passengers as they moved toward the sunlight which drenched all those out on the wharf, bright sunlight, Mediterranean sunlight.

As Alexander himself disembarked, a small group of island folk greeted him and the small group of other travellers with hand-written signs on cardboard reading 'rooms'. The Greek word 'thomatio' was one of the first words he therefore learned. He chose the oldest lady and went with her through the narrow streets lined with white-washed houses to a simple home in a garden full of mature fruit trees: peaches, pears, figs, apples and oranges. Her home reminded him of a doll's house. The old woman showed him all the rooms and he decided upon one with a glimpse of the harbour for 40 drachmas a night, which at the time was about a dollar. She brought him a Greek coffee and spoke in high-pitched fast-paced Greek interspersed with lots of smiles and gestures. As he sat sipping his coffee listening to this old woman chatter, he began to realise that his life was changing right then, right there. Greece does that to people. It changes them deep within.

He felt something he'd never felt before ... an ease, a contentment, a relaxation like no other. He had very little idea what the words being uttered from this old woman were, yet it didn't seem to matter. He finished his coffee, thanked the woman, briefly held her hand, smiled his infectious smile and said farewell. 'Yassu,' the old woman replied as Alexander walked off towards the harbour.

The ship by then had gone, the few vehicles too had dispersed and just a handful of fishermen remained, smoking hand-rolled cigarettes as they repaired their worn nets and spoke words to each other which, although Alexander didn't know it at the time, he would soon be learning. He noted their clothing, old and tattered, each man wearing a black fisherman's cap, little protection from the hot Greek sun of summer.

'Yassu,' one of the fishermen called as Alexander approached.

'Yassu,' he replied.

'Ti kanis?' another asked.

Alexander just smiled because he didn't know what 'ti kanis' meant.

The same man beckoned him over and offered him his pouch of tobacco. Alexander graciously accepted and sat on a wooden fish crate rolling his first Greek cigarette. There were half a dozen men within hearing distance all repairing or folding nets and all of them seemed to want to talk with Alexander.

'English?' one of the younger men asked.

'No, Holland,' Alexander replied.

'Speak English?' the same man attempted.

'Yes I do.'

'Where you from?'

'Holland,' he repeated.

'Hollandia,' another offered.

'Yes, yes,' answered Alexander excited that his message had got through.

'Word is neh,' the first man told him.

Neh means *no* not *yes*, Alexander thought to himself.

'Manolis,' the fisherman said, 'name Manolis,' pointing to his chest. 'You name?'

'I am Alexander.'

'Roh ... Alexander Great,' Manolis said with respect, and all the men including Alexander laughed.

'Me Polychroni,' another stated offering his hand.

Alexander shook the man's hand and one by one met the others, Michaeli, Thanassi and a couple he couldn't quite get his tongue around.

'You holiday?' Thanassi asked.

'Yes holiday,' he replied.

'Good. Tinos, plenty psarades, fish, plenty Ouzo.'

Again they laughed.

Finishing his cigarette, Alexander got up and gestured a farewell. 'Yassu,' he offered, his second word of Greek.

'Yassu,' the men called, as Alexander smiled and walked off, marvelling at the quaint Greek fishing boats tied to the side of the wharf and gobsmacked by the clarity of the water everywhere he looked. The waters of his homeland were not clear like the waters before him now that was for sure.

On his first day on the island, he simply wanted to wander around town and see what he could find. It didn't take long for him to come across a truly stunning building, the Panagia Evangelistria, the church of the Megalohari (Great Grace) where, in 1822, an icon was discovered by a nun after having been directed to it by the Blessed Virgin Mary herself who visited the nun in a dream. The icon was purported to have had miraculous powers and thus the church was built soon after. Alexander marvelled at the ornate exterior, so different to any church he'd ever seen before, and upon entering the church was blown away by the spiritual atmosphere. Chandeliers hung from the high ceilings and a thousand candles burned brightly, gently flickering with the continual opening and closing of the many doors.

He wasn't a holy person, but he knelt down anyway and was immediately cloaked in that feeling he'd experienced moments before with the old woman, a feeling he could only call contentment, but it was something more, something much more.

After a few moments of quiet contemplation he left and meandered further, through streets of houses whiter than any white he'd ever seen. Holland is such a grey and colourless place compared to this, he thought.

It didn't take long for him to reach the outskirts of the town.

The impressive jagged mountain of Exobourgo stood proud before him beckoning to be climbed. The track was bordered by stone terracing which had been constructed centuries before. A labyrinth of these paths criss-crossed the island, used by island folk to transport their produce by donkey as they had done for many centuries and still do today.

Alexander climbed for half an hour to the very top and before him lay the entire island and many others off into the distance. He noticed then that someone had been following him and was about to arrive.

'Yassu,' Alexander called after a few short moments.

'Yassu,' the man replied. 'Ti kanis?'

Alexander gestured that he didn't understand.

'It means *"How are you?"* in my language. People will ask you all the time.'

'Yes I've wondered.'

The man stopped beside Alexander and took a few deep breaths.

'If you are good, you answer *kala*, perhaps even *kala efharisto*.'

'Which is ...'

'It means good, *kala* good, *efharisto* thank you. You try.'

'Kalar efhaistro,' Alexander replied awkwardly.

'Ah is almost right. Try *kala ef-ha-risto*.'

'Kala efharisto.'

'Kala, my friend, is good. You speak good Greek. How long have you been in Greece?'

'This is my first day. I arrived in Athens this morning early.

Then I caught the first ship. It was coming here, so Tinos was my choice.'

'Good place Tinos, very good island, *poly kala*, very good.'

'Poly kala,' attempted Alexander, pleasing his new friend.

'*Pose leni?* What is your name?'

'I am Alexander.'

'Oh poly kala, Alexander the Great,' the man replied, quite impressed.

'And your name?'

'I am Polychroni.'

'I met another Polychroni today.'

'Means many years ... *poly* is many or very, *chronia* is years. So my name is many years. I am old man,' he said laughing.

Alexander thought him to be in his forties, not old at all.

'Tell me Polychroni, what islands are these?'

'Oh you see so many. In front of us here is Paros and to the left, Naxos. Beyond Paros is Ios and the furthest is Santorini ... is a clear day so can see very far, but because they are in line, you can't tell where one starts and the other finishes, *katalaven?* You understand?'

'Katalaven,' Alexander replied. He most definitely did understand.

'Hey Alexander the Great, you are kala with your Greek, poly kala!'

'And the other islands?' Alexander asked.

'Poh, we have 6,000 islands. From here you see dozens. To your right is Sifnos and Serifos, then Kythnos and in front Syros, our administrative capital and the little one, the old prison island Gyaros. Behind us Andros.'

'How many are inhabited?'

'Only two or three hundred.'

It was a lot for Alexander to take in on his first day. 'It's so beautiful here,' he said. 'You have a beautiful country.'

'Yes,' Polychroni agreed, *oreo* beautiful, *poly oreo* very beautiful.'

They sat together in quiet contemplation for a long time. Way down at the harbour a fishing boat left the port and Alexander thought it may well have been one of the fishermen he met earlier, off to catch some *psarades*.

After some time, Polychroni asked, 'So Alexander the Great, how long you plan to stay in Tinos?'

'I have no plan, perhaps a few days, perhaps longer.'

'Is good plan to have no plan. Just let happen what happens. I see you again. I go now.'

'Will I though, see you again?' Alexander asked.

'I think so, is a small island. I find you. Is no problem *endaxi?*'

'What is endaxi?'

'Endaxi means okay, endaxi?'

'Endaxi.'

'Yassu my friend.'

'Yassu Polychroni.'

Polychroni stepped down the rocks with great agility, deciding not to take the trail, but instead a shortcut. Alexander reached into his day-pack and pulled out his water bottle and a book, had a drink and started to read. It was Hermann Hesse's *Siddhartha*, and although Alexander was nearing the end of the book, he understood only parts of what he was reading. He thought to himself that perhaps he should read it again when he finished it.

He sat back with his day-pack as a pillow and continued to read. *'Gentleness is stronger than severity, water is stronger than rock, love is stronger than force.'* This made sense, but so much of what he'd read to date did not. Perhaps the reading of such books had to be done in the right place and in the right state of mind, he thought. He read on. He kept reading until he had finished the book. It was only the final thirty or so pages that he read sitting there on the mountain of

Exobourgo, but suddenly the whole book made sense, even the previously difficult-to-understand sections. The right place and state of mind was crucial, he realised. He looked in the direction of Santorini, past Paros in the foreground and Ios beyond, and felt enormously refreshed even though the afternoon sun was unrelenting. He opened the book at another page, just to see if he could remember where on the bus journey from Amsterdam he had read it, but also to see if it had a clearer meaning this time. '*It taught him how to listen – how to listen with a quiet heart and a waiting soul, open soul, without passion, without desire, without judgment, without opinion.*'

I remember reading this, he thought to himself. It was very much in the beginning of his journey, at night, near the Belgian-German border, confused and distracted by the border activity he noticed outside the bus, of armed guards. On the Belgian side they were relaxed but moments later when he reached the German border control, the guards were more authoritative and mean-looking. It was only twenty odd years since the end of the Second World War, and everyone with a uniform in Germany had kept their menacing demeanour. He compared Hesse's words on how to listen with those of one of his teachers who, years before, had said: 'We have two ears and one mouth. We should go through life using them in that proportion.' He laughed at this memory knowing well that he shouldn't compare the profound words of a great writer with those of his high school teacher.

A gentle breeze began to blow. Alexander picked up his day-pack and began the journey back to town. Unlike Polychroni, he chose the real track, rather than testing his own agility. As he walked, he started to notice all sorts of things: the aromas of the fields, rosemary growing in every nook and cranny. Even the smell of cow dung seemed beautiful. As he got closer to town he heard music. He had never heard a bouzouki before, and the beautiful sounds were mesmerising. Children were playing a game like hopscotch, laughing and screaming as he approached. Beyond the children a group of men were playing games of backgammon on the balcony of a café. Beside them, a man wearing an apron, most likely the owner, was playing the magnificent string instrument.

Alexander decided to enter the café, taking a seat just inside the main entrance where he could see and hear all that was going on.

'Yassu,' called a woman from behind the counter. 'Oreestey?'

Alexander had no idea what she was asking, but assumed she was asking him for an order. He decided to go to the counter and to see what was on offer.

'English?' she asked.

'I am from Holland,' Alexander replied.

'You want ouzo?'

'Yes please.' He thought to himself, why not!

'Endaxi, sit, I bring.'

'Efharisto,' Alexander replied.

A moment later the woman arrived with a glass of ouzo. Placing it on the table in front of him she said, 'Parakalo.'

Alexander again said the word 'Efharisto.' It was his first day and already he had a handful of words in his repertoire.

Sipping the drink he'd just ordered made him even more relaxed and together with the men playing backgammon and the bouzouki music, he decided life was pretty good. The woman then returned with a small plate of something which Alexander thought looked quite unusual. Together with a large slice of lemon, he peered inquisitively at the woman.

'Oktopous, you like, eat.'

'Kala,' he replied.

'Kala,' the woman repeated, 'yes, is good.'

Alexander squeezed the lemon onto the tiny morsels and started to eat. It was delicious. Coupled with the ouzo, it was the perfect combination. It was a little salty however, but before he could ask, the woman brought him a glass of water, saying, 'Nero, water.'

Again he said thank you, 'Efharisto,' his pronunciation of the word now almost perfect after having said it a few times.

Devouring both the octopus and gulping down the ouzo, Alexander signalled for the woman to bring more. Pointing to both items on his table, an empty plate and an empty glass, he said, 'Same please.'

'To ithio parakalo,' she said. 'Same please.'

It was getting a bit much for Alexander and with that first large ouzo making him a little drowsy, he decided to keep his Greek lessons for another day. He just sat back and enjoyed the music and the colourful vista of the port, the fishing boats and the sapphire blue waters.

Why is the water so different from back home, so beautifully blue? He wondered. In Holland, it's grey or brown but not like this, never like this. As he pondered the blue of the waters, the music stopped and the man with the apron stood up and walked inside the café.

'Hey filos, you want another ouzo?' he called.

'No thanks, I still have some left.'

'You like the octopus?'

'Absolutely. It's poly kala.'

'So you speak Greek, neh?'

Using the Greek word for yes, Alexander replied, 'Neh.' He laughed and then added, 'No not really.'

'But your Greek is good, yes?'

'I've only been here a day.'

'You speak Greek before you come?'

'No, the few words I've learned have all been taught to me today.'

'Well my friend, you pick up this language quickly.'

'Efharisto,' Alexander answered proudly. 'We Dutch do that. We're pretty good with languages.'

'How many languages you speak? Asked the owner.

'Dutch, English and German.'

'Is impressive,' replied the owner.

'You stay on Tinos long?'

'Maybe a week.'

'You will like it here. Is very good life. No crazy people. All sigah, sigah ... slowly, slowly. Why you travel? What is reason?'

'To open my eyes and my mind,' Alexander replied.

'Is good answer. Just remember one thing my friend ... seemerah, today is the first day of the rest of your life. Make it count, tomorrow too,' the man said with a smile.

Alexander thought about these words as the owner went on with his chores, chatting quietly with his wife. Make it count, he thought to himself. That should be easy.

The men continued to play backgammon and a local bus pulled up outside depositing its passengers before the driver crunched the gears and drove off.

Alexander stood up, paid his bill and gestured a goodbye calling, 'Yassu,' to the couple behind the counter, as he walked out of the café.

'Yassu,' they replied in unison.

Alexander stepped into the bright afternoon sunshine, smiling at the men playing backgammon, and slowly walked off towards his accommodation. He was in no rush.

'Hey Alexander Yassu.' It was Polychroni from the mountaintop.

'Yassu Polychroni.'

'See I told you we'd meet again. Is a small island. Hey you want to have dinner afterwards?'

'Sure,' Alexander replied. 'That'd be good. First I want to have a shower though.'

'Endaxi, we meet in an hour?'

'Yes but where?'

'Here is good.'

'Yes okay, see you back here in an hour then.'

'Endaxi,' replied Polychroni with a smile.

'Endaxi,' laughed Alexander, before walking off with a wave.

Returning to his room, he took a quick but invigorating shower, changed and headed off in the other direction in order to do a loop around the part of town he hadn't yet explored, seeing how people went about their afternoon chores, watering their plants, bringing in the washing and just sitting and resting. Then he wound up back at the port a few minutes ahead of the planned meeting time with Polychroni. The remaining fishing boats were coming in with their catch. A few townsfolk were heading down to meet them. Alexander decided just to sit with his legs dangling over the side of the promenade searching for fish as he waited.

There were fish literally everywhere. Alexander had never seen anything like it. He thought for a moment that the fishermen didn't need to go out in their boats at all. They simply needed to throw a line in from the side of the wharf. No, he thought, they must be hoping to net them in larger numbers.

Just then Polychroni approached. 'Hello my friend, yassu.'

'Yassu Polychroni.'

He sat down with Alexander and asked, 'What would you like to eat?'

'I'm happy with anything you choose.'

'Well, do you like fish?'

'I had some octopus before and it was great.'

'My sister and her husband have the best seafood restaurant on the island, so how about we go there?'

'Fine with me. Tell me Polychroni, what is your job here on the island?'

'I am a teacher.'

'What do you teach?'

'Art and history at the local high school.'

'Which do you prefer?'

'I have no preference. I have a love for them both.'

'I was never any good at history, but I love art. I carry a

sketch-pad with me everywhere I go.'

'I'd like to see some of your work. What do you like to sketch?'

'People and animals mainly, but now that I'm travelling, I'd like to draw other things as well.'

'Come on,' Polychroni started as he got to his feet, 'let's go and eat.'

Alexander hopped up and together they headed off to the restaurant. It was nearing the end of the day and the sun was about to set next to or behind the island of Syros. It remained to be seen where the sun would sink.

They arrived at the restaurant and Polychroni introduced his sister to Alexander.

'Maria, this is Alexander.'

'Yassu Alexander. Pleased to meet you.' She showed them to a seat with a view of the harbour, and brought a menu. Polychroni immediately ordered a bottle of Retsina.

It was a scrumptious dinner they ordered with Polychroni suggesting every plate. They had calamari, tzatziki, a Greek salad, saganaki and moussaka, all shared in true Greek fashion.

Over dinner Polychroni asked Alexander what his favourite pastimes were.

'Reading and riding my bicycle,' was his reply.

'What you like to read?' Polychroni inquired.

'Today on the mountain I finished reading Hermann Hesse's Siddhartha.'

'That's impressive. What's next?'

'I intended to look for a bookshop tomorrow.'

'Perhaps you will allow me to loan you a book.'

'Yes all right,' replied Alexander thankfully.

Alexander's first Greek sunset was about to happen, setting into the Mediterranean just to the north of Syros. The entire sky had turned orange.

Alexander learned that Polychroni's wife was away in Athens

visiting her sick mother, but when she was here on the island she ran the local newspaper *The Tinos Pharos*. Both of them were educated people and as Alexander ate the delicious foods and drank the unusual Retsina, he learned that these two were a lot more than just an educated couple. Polychroni had taught at prestigious institutions both in Greece and abroad and his wife was a published author. Alexander looked forward to meeting her. He asked when she might return to the island.

'Within a few days, I expect,' replied Polychroni. 'Her mother is improving every day.'

'That's good to hear,' Alexander stated sympathetically.

'Tell me,' started Polychroni, 'what's the real reason that you're travelling? Surely at your age you should be doing national service.'

'That's true. I'm escaping my responsibilities.'

'You do realise, I suppose, that you'll have to stay away from your country for quite some years. Your government won't want you back without some form of punishment.'

'Yes I do realise this fact.'

'So what are you going to do?'

'Travel and keep travelling, I suppose.'

'Do you think that's wise?'

'It's worrying not being able to go back and see my family and friends, but we can meet for holidays in countries near and far from Holland, and that's exactly what we'll be doing I presume.'

'It's not ideal though, is it? Do you have another choice?'

'Not really,' answered Alexander sadly. 'I'm a pacifist, and the alternative service option is no real option at all. I don't want to spend eighteen months of my life doing something I sincerely don't want to do.'

'But aren't your options things like helping the ambulance service or assisting at a primary or preschool?'

'Yes but I don't even want to do that.'

'Good luck then, my friend. You're going to need it.'

The twilight sky was now turning to deep purple. The Retsina was taking effect. Alexander felt quite drowsy. 'I'm going to have to call it a night. I haven't slept properly for three days.

'I completely understand,' replied Polychroni.

'I'll call for the bill,' said Alexander.

'You most certainly will not. I will pay. My sister owns the restaurant. I get a good deal.'

'Well thank you very much. It's been a superb meal and it's been great getting to know you.'

'Let's continue this talk tomorrow. Would you like to?'

'Yes actually I would,' stated Alexander emphatically.

'And I'll bring a book or two, something I think you'd like to read.'

'I'd appreciate that, thanks.'

'And you can show me your drawings.'

'No problem.'

'Kalinikta Alexander.' *Kalinikta* is Good night.'

'Kalinikta Polychroni.'

They shook hands and parted company.

Alexander walked home slowly. The first stars of night were now visible. Just a soft glow remained in the western sky. The sounds of a Greek village gently bombarded his ears: dogs barking in the distance, conversations in Greek here and there, the chores of washing up being performed, the sound of a motorbike with a faulty muffler in the distance.

That night Alexander slept like a baby. He woke not long after sunrise and decided the best way to start the day was to have a swim. He walked down to a stretch of sand he'd noticed when he met the fishermen the day before and plunged in without hesitation. It was his first swim since last summer and it was a beautiful feeling. Even here in the harbour there were fish everywhere. After a long time in the water, Alexander dried off and went to find somewhere for breakfast. He was well aware that he had to watch his money. While finishing high school he held down two jobs, one assisting in his mother's bakery and the other in a local bicycle repair shop. Together with a substantial gift from his grandparents and parents he had enough money to last him a year, maybe longer if he was careful. His entire family including his two sisters were sympathetic with him not wanting to join the army. The older members of the family knew war well. Nearly everyone in Europe had been affected by the loss of someone close.

He sat down at another of the many harbourside cafés and ordered his breakfast. As he had nothing to read he just watched the world go by. It wasn't until several hours later that he ran into Polychroni.

'Here, I have a couple of books for you to read. Both of them are by the author Krishnamurti.'

Alexander excitedly accepted the books. 'Thanks very much. Who is this author?'

'Krishnamurti is one of the greatest thinkers of the twentieth century,' replied Polychroni. 'His views on life, God, the seeking of pleasure, relationships and so much more have encouraged many others from all corners of the world during his life and since to go within and seek answers to the complexities of life. If you, Alexander, are the type of person to read Hermann Hesse, then you will appreciate the writings of Krishnamurti, I am sure. I loan you these two books in the hope that they will affect you as they did me.'

Opening the first book, Alexander got that same feeling again. He looked Polychroni straight in the eye and said, 'I can honestly feel that what I am holding here is enormously special. I thank you from the bottom of my heart.'

'Say no more. Enjoy the reading. Now might I see some of your sketches?'

'Sure,' Alexander replied as he reached for his sketch-pad and handed it to Polychroni.

'These are excellent,' said Polychroni as he viewed each of the dozen or so drawings. 'You have a very unique style.'

'Thank you,' Alexander replied pleased to get the compliment.

'Reading and art and travelling the world ... an admirable combination.'

With those words Polychroni turned to leave. 'Yassu Alexander. Enjoy the books.'

'Yassu, efharisto.'

The days ahead for Alexander were astonishing. Never before in his life had he read such meaningful words. Of course being 19 years of age, it was an extraordinarily influential time of a young man's life, and reading Krishnamurti opened Alexander's mind like never before.

Krishnamurti described things that Alexander found both moving and disturbing. Sometimes he understood every word on a page. Other times he became confused, even annoyed at what he was reading, annoyed because his mind seemed so limited. He'd often arrive at dead ends. He walked around the whole island with these life-changing books. He read passages and whole chapters on hilltops, headlands and beaches. He made notes of his favourite passages, some from the books themselves, and others from the notes that Polychroni had placed perhaps as bookmarks of his own favourite passages. 'Truth is a pathless land. There is no guide, no law, and no tradition which will lead you to it but your own constant and intelligent awareness,' one read.

In just three days Alexander had devoured the first book loaned to him by Polychroni, titled 'This Matter of Culture'. Immediately he began the next book. He'd not seen Polychroni for days. He'd now been on the island nearly a week. The realisation of the right book in the right frame of mind and in the right location became even more evident as he read page after page of this great writer's thoughts. Upon reading the final page, Alexander again experienced that sublime contentment.

His mind was racing with ideas and thoughts, but he was exceptionally relaxed.

Almost as if on cue, Polychroni arrived on Alexander's doorstep less than an hour after Alexander had finished the second book. 'How are you Alexander?' he asked as he reached out and offered his hand.

'I am particularly well,' was his reply. 'Have a seat.'

'Have you enjoyed the books?'

'I have just this morning finished the second one, and yes I've enjoyed them immensely.'

'What have you learned?'

'I've learned that I must keep reading so as to learn more.'

'A very wise thing to say. What are your next plans?'

'I will leave soon and travel to other islands. Has your wife returned yet?'

'No, her mother has taken a turn for the worse. She feels she must stay in Athens for a while longer.'

'That's a shame. I probably won't get to meet her.'

'Perhaps next time Alexander. Most people who come to Tinos return one day.'

'I certainly hope I do. But I think it's time to move on. The world is a big place and I don't just want to visit Greece.'

'Where else would you like to travel?'

'Having read a little of Krishnamurti, I think I'd like to go to India after here.'

'But first Santorini, yes?'

'Paros, then Santorini.'

'I'll give you some books to travel with. I'll drop them by tomorrow. What day might you leave?'

'Probably the day after tomorrow. There's a ship leaving that day for Paros.'

'Endaxi Alexander. Then we must have a farewell dinner tomorrow, yes?'

'That would be great.'

'I'll see you first thing in the morning with the books. What time do you rise?'

'Usually a little after the sun comes up.'

'See you then, yassu.'

'Yassu Polychroni, and thanks again.'

Alexander spent the rest of the day in contemplation. He certainly had plenty to think about. His biggest concern ever since he received his papers to go into the army, was war itself and the absolute insanity of the human species to involve itself in war. He thought long and hard while he was completing his high-school studies as to the best choice for a conscientious objector and in the end decided quite simply to hit the road. He didn't think he was escaping. He just wanted to find his real self and somehow be of good to his fellow man. Always popular at school, his decision to travel was not looked upon favourably by his fellow students. Yet his closest friend, Thomas, supported him 100 percent. Now in this semi-remote Greek island, Alexander felt his decision was the right one.

Next morning shortly after sunrise Polychroni arrived with several books.

'What have we got here?' asked Alexander, keen to find out.

'A few books this time. I know you're travelling and books are heavy so what we have here is a very select group. Handing them to Alexander almost ceremoniously and one by one, he said, 'Firstly a book called *The Prophet* by Khalil Gibran, then *The Republic* by Plato, and this one I'm sure you'll like, Hesse's *Narcissus & Goldmund*, George Orwell's *1984*, Dante Alighieri's *The Divine Comedy* and finally Aldous Huxley's *Brave New World*. It gave me enormous pleasure to put together this handful of titles. Alexander I have literally thousands of good books, some of them quite exceptional as I'm sure you'll agree after reading this second group. These are your books to keep or to pass on to whoever you think might be a worthy recipient.'

'Efharisto a thousand times over, Polychroni. Again I can feel in my hands and my heart that what you have given me here is more than special. There is just so much,' he said, almost shocked at the number.

'Remember my friend, it's not the quantity of books you read, but the quality.'

'Of course.'

'Now if you return to Tinos at any time, and I sincerely hope you do, I have many more books for you to read. So, back to normal things, where would you like to eat tonight?'

'Your sister's place,' Alexander started, 'but I want to pay,' he added emphatically.

'We'll see. Now I must go and work. I have some private tutoring today.'

'See you later then.'

'Yassu Alexander.'

Again Alexander started to read as soon as Polychroni was out the door. As was often the case with Alexander and a pile of books, he would first read a few lines or flick through reading a little of each book before deciding which one he would start with. That was the case again with this group. In the end he chose Hesse's *Narcissus and Goldmund*. He sat back on a wicker chair in the partial sunshine, a bottle of water beside him and began to read.

Hours later feeling the effects of the sun, he went inside to lie down. His mind was racing. His physics teacher in his final year of high school told him one very important fact and that was that the brain is the most complicated kilogram of matter in the universe. He was finally understanding what his teacher meant. His brain actually hurt from the input.

Alexander found it absolutely astonishing to be able to absorb all that he was reading, or at least most of what he was reading.

He had never considered himself particularly intelligent but in his final two years of high school he'd received better results in his exams that he had in all the previous ten years of schooling. Clutching Hesse's book to his chest as he lay on his bed, he felt confident that he had the personality as well as the intellect to comprehend almost anything which had been given to him by his Greek friend. He was excited to say the least at what lay ahead. This is my first week of travel, he thought to himself. 'I have already read books by Hermann Hesse and Krishnamurti,' he said to himself. 'I have in my possession several others, all of which I presume are equally mind-expanding.' With a plan to travel further within the cradle of civilisation and beyond to countries like India, he was sure his knowledge could even grow exponentially.

'Alexander,' his landlady called.

Alexander jumped up and walked to the door. His landlady had a bowl of fruit, freshly picked and cut as well as a glass of orange juice. 'Parakalo,' she said handing them to him.

Perfect he thought, just what I need. 'Efharisto.'

The old woman smiled, turned and walked away saying something incomprehensible. Alexander was overjoyed and immediately began to eat and drink. With all the reading, he'd completely forgotten to have lunch. The fruit and juice were delicious, just like everything else in Greece.

A few moments after he'd finished eating, he was dozing peacefully. An ever so gentle afternoon breeze blew through his open door. It was another extremely hot afternoon and everyone on the island would be glad to have this breeze. Very few could afford the luxury of air-conditioning.

Alexander slept like this for an hour or more. When he woke up he was feeling quite refreshed. He looked at his watch and noticed that it was nearly 4 o'clock, so he decided to go down for a swim. As always it was a good idea because when he came out of the water he was even more refreshed. Two small children, probably brother and sister, played with a beach-ball supervised by their overweight mother. 'Yassu,' she called.

'Yassu,' Alexander replied. The little ones called out 'yassu' also.

That evening Alexander and Polychroni again enjoyed dinner at Maria's restaurant. They had a completely different array of food, but it was as enjoyable as the first time. These two souls who were years apart in age but similar in so many other ways talked until all the restaurant guests had left. They talked about the books Polychroni had given to Alexander and about subjects the likes of which Alexander had never spoken to anyone about. It was an evening of enlightenment.

'If you travel to India, Alexander, you will come across ashrams and centres of learning like nowhere else on earth. Travel slowly. Stay in one place more than moving around. If you feel comfortable or inquisitive in a new location, stay there and see what happens.'

'Alright,' he replied simply.

'I really hope you come back Alexander. Come back and visit again. Meet my wife. Search through my library. You are welcome anytime.'

'I know I'm welcome, and yes I think I will return. Thanks for everything.'

With that, they said good night. 'I'll come and see you off on the ship tomorrow.'

'I look forward to that. Good night. Kalinikta.'

'Kalinikta Alexander.'

The next morning, as Alexander was walking towards the port, he heard the ship's horn blow from a distance before he saw the ship itself. Polychroni was waiting for him on the wharf.

'It's been an absolute pleasure meeting you Polychroni,' Alexander stated emphatically.

'The pleasure's been all mine,' replied Polychroni.

Within minutes, the ship had dropped anchor and was reversing into the wharf. Polychroni embraced his young friend. 'Do return, please.'

'Thank you for everything. I think my rucksack has some exceptional knowledge contained in it. Meeting you has changed me a lot. All the opinions and knowledge of the world is contained inside the covers of books. My journey to discover this has now begun thanks to you. Yassu.'

With that the two parted and Alexander boarded the ship with a small group of others. He climbed to the aft deck and waved to Polychroni who in turn waved back.

Then the ship blew its horn, ropes were loosened by the fishermen on the wharf, the engine revs increased and the ship pulled slowly away.

CHAPTER TWO

The wind had come up early and the ship gently rode the small swell out of the harbour. Alexander could see fishing boats dotted all over the place, men busily pulling in nets with little mechanical assistance. The smaller fishing boats bobbed around quite boisterously on the increased off-shore swell.

Alexander chose a bench out of the wind and sat to continue his book, peering up one last time to view the port as the ship rounded the southern headland and the town dropped out of sight.

Even though it was nearing the middle of summer, the ship was by no means crowded. Alexander settled down to read until they were nearing Paros, a journey of just a few hours. He read and read, excitedly turning page after page soon realising the similarity between Goldmund and himself. He wondered if this was the reason Polychroni had given him this particular book but thought it more likely that the reason was that it was simply a very good read. He started to wonder what all the other books he'd been given were about and was looking forward to each with anticipation.

By early afternoon the island of Paros was coming into view. Waves crashed on the tiny rocky outcrops off the harbour entrance and the Meltemi winds blew the spray far into the air. As the ship rounded the northern point, Alexander noticed a beautiful little whitewashed church and the ruins of a building nearby. I'd like to make that my first sketch here, he thought to himself.

Within minutes the ship had blown its horn, dropped anchor

and was reversing into the dock. He packed away his book, and headed down to disembark. Again a group of locals greeted the passengers with handwritten signs advertising their hotels and rooms. This time however Alexander decided to search for a place without assistance. He wanted to be right overlooking the water this time and ended up choosing a quaint little room upstairs from a café and a stone's throw from the water. He had to share the bathroom with the other guests but his room was just perfect. From the pillow of his bed he could see the harbour entrance and the pretty little church that he planned as his first sketch. Paros, he considered on his first afternoon on the island, was even more beautiful than Tinos.

His first few days on the island were filled with discovery. He did take his Hesse book with him, but spent more time learning about the history of the island, of the Crusades and the Ottoman era, of the high-quality Parian marble said to have been used in the construction of the Venus de Milo. Whilst wandering around Parikea on his first afternoon, he found the church of a hundred doors, Panagia Ekatontapiliani, parts of which are 1,600 years old and just like the church on Tinos, Panagia Evangelistria, he felt compelled to enter and explore. He was beginning to realise how resplendent all these major churches in Greece were.

Later that afternoon he put in a call to his mother back in Holland. He'd promised to call her regularly and thought that once a month was sufficient. He told her all the news: where he'd been, where he was planning to go next, even what he was reading. She told him that all the family was fine and each and every one of them was missing him. He promised to call again in a few weeks but in the meantime if she wanted to send a written message to Poste Restante Santorini, he'd be happy to receive it.

On his second day he set off around the harbour to the tiny church he'd noticed from the ship. Sketch-pad, pencils and charcoal in his day pack, he walked around the waterfront, over hills and along beaches to his destination just over an hour's walking distance. Seated in the shade of a tree he sketched in great detail the tiny whitewashed church. Birds visited him, boats passed by and the wind remained a constant gentle breeze. When he finished, he was very happy with the result.

Returning by the same route, he plunged into the waters of the harbour again and again. By the time he got back to Parikea, he was quite thirsty. I mustn't forget to take my water bottle next time, he thought. He chose to sit at a café prominently positioned next to the wharf. With so many locals enjoying their Greek coffee and conversation, the 'Harbour Café' seemed the place to be. Several octopuses hung on the awning railing in the afternoon sun, a sight that Alexander was soon to get used to. When the waiter arrived he ordered a Greek coffee and took out his book. He stayed there an hour or so reading and ordering a second coffee.

Parikea seemed considerably busier than Tinos had been. A nearby taxi rank with battered old Russian and Australian cars offered trips to locations that the few buses didn't get to. Alexander took note of the possible destinations as buses came and went. He wanted to explore further afield the next day.

When tomorrow came he chose the bus to Naoussa, a small fishing village on the north side of the island. The journey was only about half an hour but the rickety old bus rumbled and shook the whole trip. On arrival he was greeted by an extremely quiet town square surrounded by tiny shops and cafés. As there were a few trees offering shade, he chose to sit and read. Ordering an apple juice he took out his book and continued on from where he had left off earlier.

When the waitress returned with his drink he noticed a beautiful young lady sitting several tables away. How gorgeous, he thought to himself. I wonder if she'll look in my direction. He was really taken by her beauty. Brilliantly blonde hair, adorable skin slightly sunburned, strikingly deep blue eyes and cute farmer's overalls. Just then she got up and walked off. Alexander felt compelled to follow her. A bicycle parked nearby leaning against one of the trees beckoned him. He looked around for the owner and, when he found him, offered a single finger indicating a one minute loan, and called *efharisto* as he rode off. Just outside the town limits he caught up with her.

'Hello,' he began. 'Are you on holiday?'

'Yes, I am,' she replied with a fascinating accent.

'Where are you from?'

'From Bavaria.'

'Have you been on Paros long?'

'Just over a month,' she replied with a hint of annoyance.

'Could we meet later for a drink?'

'Yes, if you want,' she replied rather unenthusiastically.

'Are you staying in Parikea?'

'Yes, near the windmill at the end of the harbour.'

'Okay, I'll find you I'm sure. Bye.'

As he rode off, he was horrified at how stupid he must have sounded. Back at the café he found it difficult to read. His mind was almost entirely on the young lady. I didn't even ask her name, he realised. I hope I find her later.

He spent the day exploring Naoussa and the surrounding countryside. I could live here, he thought to himself. At the end of the day he caught the bus back to the other side of the island and immediately began searching for the pretty lady. He hung around the windmill with his book pretending to read. Then he had dinner at a restaurant close by in the hope that she would walk past. He waited hours but he didn't catch sight of her. Hours after the sun had set and after several attempts walking the streets near the windmill to no avail, he decided to call it a night. Feeling quite despondent, he walked back slowly to this room.

In bed with a half-moon shining upon the harbour waters, he

couldn't sleep. He lay awake thinking of her, what her likes and dislikes might be, what music she might like, what books she might read, or if she liked books at all.

The next day, after a difficult night of little sleep, Alexander chose to again start the day with a swim. On the way down to the beach, he saw somebody who resembled the blonde lady from the day before, softly playing a guitar sitting in the sand. Sure enough as he got closer he discovered it was her.

'Hi,' he called excitedly as he approached.

'Hello,' she replied.

'Can I sit with you?'

'Of course, but can you sing?'

'No,' Alexander replied cautiously. 'Don't let me interrupt you though.'

She continued to play and sing, and Alexander with his limited knowledge of music, guessed the piece to be Bob Dylan's *How Many Roads.*

'That was beautiful,' he said when she finished.

'Thanks, it's a pity you don't sing or play also. Would you like to go in the water?'

'First I'd like to know your name.'

'It's Barbara.'

'And I'm Alexander.'

'Come on, let's swim Alexander.'

This was something quite new for him. Alexander had never been swimming with a girl before, apart from his younger sisters but not a girl like this. He'd also never been on a beach with a girl playing guitar before. As they swam together, he felt quite excited.

They spent the day together, talking, playing music, swimming more. Barbara even got him to sing with her. After dinner that evening he invited her back to his room. They talked for hours, sitting on his bed and later they made love into the early hours, passionate and intense.

The following day was all music and conversation. Barbara played the most delicate and sublime music. The guitar she used was on loan from another traveller, and not a very good guitar at that.

'You must be astonishing on a decent guitar,' he told her.

'Thank you, I play a lot. Music is extremely important to me. I love to play. My father taught me that music is an international language. Even the word music, musik, musique says this. Music travels in many forms he says ... it is the soft subtle notes of a mandolin, the voice of a young child, the wind in the trees and so many other things.'

'I couldn't agree more. I don't play any instrument but I'd love to. Perhaps in my travels I'll discover an instrument that I'd like to learn to play.'

Alexander remained on Paros for some weeks spending most of his time with Barbara. After he finished Hesse's *Narcissus and Goldmund,* he took a rest from reading. Instead while Barbara played guitar he sketched. Sometimes with pencils, other times with crayon and charcoal he would sketch Barbara's hands as they played the instrument, her exquisite face as she constructed a musical piece, the faces of other people who walked by, animals in the fields, donkeys in particular. He sketched more churches, fences—the stone ones which separated the fields—and he sketched flowers and herbs. He drew fishing boats, their nets and paraphernalia in great detail, all the while enjoying the special music offered by Barbara. His favourite sketches though were of her.

They became close during these weeks. He presented his new love with a drawing nearly every day. She was appreciative and brought him flowers and ouzo. Having been on the island much longer than he had, she knew where to get the best brew. Next door and downstairs from the post office, there was a tiny Ouzo and Raki shop. The owner made it himself at his home not far out of town. It was by far the best ouzo around.

They made love nearly every day. He asked her to travel with him, but she refused. He tried to persuade her continually, but she stood her ground.

'I must return to Germany,' she would say. 'I need to study music and to make it my life.'

He could see that the two of them would be able to get closer given the chance, but every time he raised the question of travelling together, she said no.

Before summer was over they parted company, Barbara returning to Germany as planned and Alexander sailing off to Santorini. For days after they went their separate ways, Alexander was devastated. He had hoped she would join him even if only for a short time. But it was not to be. They didn't even exchange addresses, not that Alexander had one, but she would have, and he'd neglected to ask.

On Santorini Alexander continued his exploration admiring the steep cliffs of the main town, the island's volcanic history and the picture postcard architecture. After a few days of being morose he shook himself out of his misery and started getting back to his normal self. He had toyed with the idea of starting to read Khalil Gibran's *The Prophet*, mainly because it was a smaller book than the others Polychroni had given him, so he settled down one afternoon and began to read it. He didn't really get into this one, but he knew it must have some importance so he battled on. Perhaps his mind was elsewhere. His thoughts often returned to the times he'd had with Barbara, but in time, he thought of her less often. One day he remembered that he had told his mother weeks before to write to him here. He immediately ran over to the post office where sure enough there were two letters from her waiting for him.

He opened them excitedly and read all the news of the family, the ups and downs, the increased summer trade of both family businesses, his sisters' exam results, all sorts of interesting stuff. He was overjoyed to have received the letters and immediately went back inside the post office to call home.

His mother reminded him that he'd said he'd phone more often. 'Yes I'm sorry, I will,' he promised.

'Where are you going to next, darling?' his mother inquired.

'No idea Mum,' he lied. He didn't think she could cope with knowing he was off to India, best to leave that news until he arrived there.

A few days later that's where he was heading, leaving Santorini on another ship, back to Athens to arrange a visa and off to New Delhi before the end of the week. While in Athens he visited the Acropolis and of course the Parthenon, drank ouzo in Syntagma Square each afternoon and was sad that he was leaving when he eventually boarded the plane to India. He had absolutely adored the Greek islands and he thought the mainland was pretty good too. His best memory though was of his time with Barbara.

India became a true eye-opener immediately. Everything was so different from what he had grown to know in Europe. Landing in New Delhi at midnight provided Alexander with various challenges. He was still only 19 and the lack of organisation, the dirt, the way the people spoke English and the fact that it was midnight confronted a tired Alexander tremendously.

Luckily another traveller offered to share a taxi with him. The man knew exactly where he was going and told Alexander that there were hotels of all description and price range within a minute or two walk of where he himself was planning to stay. They travelled together to the centre of town and sure enough Alexander found an appropriate hotel right across the road for 20 rupees a night. He fell into bed enormously tired and slept for ten straight hours.

It was even hotter than the Greek islands when he climbed

out of bed next morning. Without air-conditioning his room was almost unbearable. He ventured out into the foyer and asked the man at the front desk where he would suggest a good place to eat. The man suggested a restaurant on the next block, so Alexander sauntered off in the direction he was told. It was a good choice, but sitting there beside the road with the hustle and bustle of New Delhi and the incessant horn blowing, the scene began to drive him crazy. So this is the land that the great Mahatma Gandhi called home, he thought, a little unimpressed. It was hot, humid, noisy and dusty. After the cleanliness of the Greek islands, it also seemed very dirty.

It wasn't long though before he fell in love with the place. He regularly took out his sketch-pad and drew what he saw. At first it was the architecture that beckoned him to put pencil to paper, but in the months that followed he drew all sorts of things: men pulling rickshaws, women in colourful saris, the sacred cows in unexpected places and close-up details of the striking faces of the inhabitants of this enchanting country. He was expanding his repertoire enormously.

Alexander spent the next year in India. He turned 20 in Pondicherry and was there at the birth of Auroville in February of that year when 5,000 people descended on the area from 124 countries with the dream of creating a new consciousness and a place to call home, free of government, crime and even money ... a different world indeed from that which the British had wanted to create in India, a little Victorian world in a foreign land where they subjugated the people.

By this time he'd read all the books which Polychroni had given him and at Auroville passed the remaining ones on to other people, sometimes swapping them for other extraordinarily good reads. To have read the works of authors like Hermann Hesse, Krishnamurti, Khalil Gibran, Plato, George Orwell, Dante Alighieri and Aldous Huxley in locations like the Greek Islands and India was extraordinary in itself, but to have done so at age 19 and 20 was remarkable.

In Pondicherry he read extensively. He became immersed in Indian culture, reading up on the life of Mahatma Ghandi, Jawaharlal Nehru, Dr Sarvepalli Radhakrishnan and others. Everyone knew of the works and life of Ghandi and Nehru, but few knew of the outstanding contributions to philosophical thought presented to the world by Radhakrishnan. So respected and revered was he, that the renowned English scholar H.N. Spalding insisted after attending lectures by Radhakrishnan that he initiate a chair at Oxford University in honour of Eastern Religions and Ethics. But these three great thinkers were not the only ones Alexander studied. Swami Vivekananda had written: *'We are what our thoughts have made us; so take care about what you think. Words are secondary; they travel far.'* Nagarjuna, whom he also read carefully, was considered to be the most influential Buddhist after Gautama Buddha himself. There was also Sri Aurobindo who lived and died in Pondicherry where he developed a method of spiritual practice called *Integral Yoga.* Alexander devoured books at an astonishing rate.

He spent months in the region and fell in love with the French colonial architecture. He spent long hours discussing complicated subjects with people from many countries and diverse backgrounds. He studied yoga and meditation in several locations throughout India and when he went across the border into Nepal for a short time, dabbled in mysticism and Buddhism. He'd grown his hair long and started smoking lots of ganja with other like-minded people. Returning to India, their music became another potent ingredient in his existence. The sitar was his favourite, but the unusual sounds of the snake charmer's pungi, the bansuri and the pulluvan pattu were all exotic instruments that captivated Alexander especially when under the influence of drugs, which in time, got a bit of a hold on him.

He took journeys to the south of Tamil Nadu to Kerala and further to Goa on the west coast, always open to conversation and continually finding places of solitude where he could meditate, which of course in India would be hard for some, but not for him.

One evening in Goa, a town known for its alternative folk and alternative ways, he was offered LSD, but it was the only time he went that far. Being chased by the trees of the forest on his way home was too much for him to endure. It took days before he returned to reality. Ganja was a peaceful drug, hashish too, both relaxing and certainly mind-expanding enough for him.

In most of the towns and cities he visited on this second journey through India, he practised yoga and as time went on smoked less and less, reserving this indulgence for special times only, not every day as it was fast becoming.

By now he had met literally hundreds of people, many of them absolutely fascinating, some of them quite unique. He'd discussed subjects that were as intriguing to him as they were to the people with whom he spoke, subjects that were often diverse. He surprised even himself sometimes with the words that came out of his mouth. With each book he read and with each conversation he had, he was gaining wisdom.

There were times when the talks were nothing more than that, just talks, but occasionally, as time went on, they became a lot more.

Only on rare occasions did he call home these days. He drifted further and further from his roots. When he *did* call, his parents voiced their disappointment in him. But this did not concern him. He simply wanted to learn as much as possible in his travels and a connection with back home thwarted that.

Reading good books, meeting fascinating people, visiting exotic locations and keeping his eyes, ears and mind open at all times were his main priorities. And he was succeeding in his aim. He remembered his favourite quote from Mahatma Gandhi:

'You must be the change you wish to see in the world'. He felt that the changes going on inside him, the absolute catharsis he was experiencing were evidence of him being that change.

It was now 1969 and man had just set foot on the moon. The world was changing for the whole human race. Alexander had travelled extensively through India on two occasions, before and after his time in Nepal. Now he felt it was time to move on. He was in Jaipur and had made the decision to travel to Kashmir, after having talked with other travellers who had come from there. To get there though he would have to catch a bus to New Delhi, then on to Islamabad, the recently constructed capital of Pakistan and finally across the border to Srinagar, referred to as the Venice of the East. He was excited to get to his destination but not for the journey getting there.

The various bus journeys and border crossings were a real pain. By the time he reached Islamabad, Alexander could go no further without rest, so he booked into a hotel which he named Cockroach Inn. They were everywhere, even in the bed. Needless to say he didn't get the sleep he wanted, and mid-way through the night he just had to do something. He took all the sheets off, shook them violently and got a foul smelling mosquito coil from the man at reception, although a reception it was not, and a mozzie coil it was also not. In between waking and thinking that the hotel was on fire and a bit of restless sleep, the hours passed until the muezzin called the worshippers to prayer at the ungodly hour of 4.30 am. Alexander woke with a start, cursed the incessant howling, but was so tired that he thankfully fell back to sleep within minutes ... at last a deep restful sleep.

CHAPTER THREE

The following day he was on the road again on the final leg to Srinagar. It was a relatively short journey and one which was quite enjoyable for a change. The bus wasn't full and even though there were a lot of chickens and a goat up the front of the bus, it was a relaxed trip, with no hiccups. The other passengers engaged him in conversation, some of whom he understood, others not. It was certainly an eclectic mix of people and animals.

Arriving in Srinagar, Alexander was gobsmacked by the natural beauty of the place as the bus drove in through the outer suburbs. It was early in the day and shadows were long. The city was located on the shores of Dal Lake and the Jhelum River with tree-covered hills in nearly every direction. He was so glad to have been told about the place. Word of mouth was the most reliable way to find things out about one's planned route.

The city is known for its migratory birds and its beautiful gardens, and everywhere he looked he saw either birds or flowers. In summer, lotus blossoms cover entire sections of the lake, but in winter in vast contrast, the temperature drops way below zero. He was looking forward more than any other city he'd visited recently, to thoroughly explore everything on offer here, the lakes, the mountains, the parks and of course to meet the people.

The bus pulled up in the centre of town and Alexander immediately began to search for a place to stay. This was his destination for the time being. After this he had no set plans, no timetable, nowhere to be except right here in Kashmir.

This is just how he liked to travel, with no plans. He was reminded of Hesse's words: *'The first small town on the southern side of the mountains. Here the true life of wandering begins, the life I love, wandering without any special direction, taking it easy in sunlight, the life of a vagabond wholly free. I am much inclined to live from my rucksack, and let my trousers fray as they like.'*

He walked slowly, inspecting the simple shop windows, checked what the street vendors were selling and noticed the many horse-drawn carts and pull-rickshaws. Throughout his meanderings he stopped and checked out an occasional boarding house, eventually choosing one to his liking, and went inside. He paid for three nights then climbed up two flights of stairs to his room and happily unpacked his gear. He walked out onto the balcony and was amazed at the view. In the foreground was the commercial district with quaint homes, marshy wetlands and lakes beyond. In the far distance and surrounding the entire valley in which all this was located were the Himalayas. It was autumn, the driest time of the year and the peaks revealed the last of the previous winter snows. It was a gorgeous setting. Alexander breathed in the mountain air clear and crisp. There was little motorised transport of any kind here, so the clean air of the mountains cloaked the city.

A knock on the door startled him briefly and intrigued, he went to see who was there. When he opened the door he was greeted by another traveller. 'Hallo,' the young man began. 'I saw you arrive.'

'Hi,' answered Alexander.

'Do you want to come to the market with me? I thought you might like to see some of what I've discovered. I've been here two days. Would you like to join me?'

'Sure, I'll just get some things.'

'Bring your camera, if you have one.'

'No I don't own one. How far is the market?'

'Half an hour walk.'

'Fine let's go. I'm Alexander by the way.'

'I'm Johannes.'

'Where are you from?'

'Germany, and you?'

'Holland.'

'Where did you come from today?'

'Islamabad and before that India.'

They went downstairs and out into the gentle hustle and bustle of Srinagar. Greeting them immediately were the soft noises of traders doing deals, of horses neighing, of shop-owners sweeping away the dust and dirt from their entrances, of children playing on the way to school.

'The market is best early in the day after the first prayers,' Johannes started, 'when the mists of dawn are slowly burning off. But it's good all morning,' he added.

'Hey Johannes, thanks for inviting me,' said Alexander gratefully.

They walked through the streets for a good half hour before reaching the shores of the lake. A misty sun was making feeble attempts at breaking through. It was a cool morning and there were boats everywhere, some laden with vegetables, others with naan, and a few, mostly paddled by women, with assortments of colourful flowers. The women wore multi-coloured saris and had beautiful earrings and necklaces and head-ware adorned with exquisite silver jewellery with many intricate designs. Alexander knew immediately that he had to return here to draw. The absorbing activity of this lakeside market and the vibrant colours set the scene for what Alexander considered to be the best place he'd yet discovered in which to draw.

It was the most beautiful setting, Alexander thought, and being from Holland he felt he knew all about canals and waterways, but what he discovered here was simply out of this world.

'Do you find this easy to take in or a bit overwhelming, Johannes?' he asked his new friend.

'A little, yeah, but not much anymore. You mean culture shock, do you?'

'No, not exactly culture shock. I mean do you get a sense of the utter diversity from one country to the next?'

'Well, as I've come overland pretty much the whole way from Germany to here, nothing surprises me anymore. I'm now used to the cultural differences as I travel, and surely you're the same.'

'Oh definitely. I often wonder what people are talking about when they refer to culture shock.'

'How long were you in India?'

'Over a year.'

'Mmm,' uttered Johannes, 'and before that?'

'The Greek Islands for a few months.'

'Then this should be normal by now.'

'Yeah, it is, but I wonder a lot about the Europeans, the Americans and so on who I see in my travels and I can actually understand why some of them are from time to time in shock. Before they travelled they didn't understand the absolute diversity they were going to experience. Hop on a plane for, say, six hours in any direction in the world and life can be totally different at the other end, totally different,' he emphasised. 'In this city for example, to get around they still use horses to pull carts, men to pull rickshaws. Here at the market, they paddle little boats, grow all their own produce and trade with each other on the water. They're not simply a century behind us, they're a world apart.'

'Is it a better world in your opinion?'

'I'm beginning to think it is. India was so spiritual. I think this whole region thrives on their beliefs. There's so much support within the family and the extended family. In our world everything's falling apart. We don't have this family support network anywhere near as strong as what I've seen for the past year and a half. Even in Greece, although it was nothing like here, it was totally different to life in Western Europe.'

'Yeah, you're right,' Johannes agreed.

'We're losing touch in the West, and I feel it's only going to get worse,' Alexander admitted sadly.

'Tell me Alexander, did you do your military service?'

'No, I don't believe in it. What about you?'

'Yes, I've just finished, but I did eighteen months with the Red Cross as an alternative.'

'What was that like?'

'It was very positive. I felt I did a lot of good. And I actually put away a little money so that I could do this trip.'

'So you also don't believe in fighting?' Alexander asked.

'Not one little bit,' Johannes replied. 'It feels like the whole world wants to be at war. We've got Vietnam, Southern Africa, the Kurdish revolt in Iran, trouble zones all over the world it seems.'

'And that's not to mention places like the Philippines, Malaysia, Israel, Nigeria and a lot more.'

'I don't want one little bit to do with any of it,' Johannes stated firmly.

'Neither do I,' Alexander added equally as emphatically.

'Come on, let's not talk doom and gloom. Do you want to buy anything?'

'Yes, let's.'

They wandered from boat to boat choosing a few fruits and vegetables, bargaining as best they could. Johannes took photos of the women in all their regalia, asking permission before doing so.

'Why don't you have a camera?' inquired Johannes.

'I just don't own one,' Alexander replied. 'And actually I like to sketch, to draw the things that appeal to me.'

'I have no skill whatsoever in drawing or painting.'

'Have you tried?'

'I was hopeless in art at school.'

'I've discovered that nearly everyone has some form of artistic skill, whether it's with pencil, paint, craft, sculpture—there's all sorts of methods.'

'Well I have my photography.'

'Yes that's another one,' Alexander agreed. 'Do you use slide film or print?'

'Print only and I do my own processing back home.'

'Ah you are into it then.'

'Yeah, I suppose you're right. Listen I'm only here for two more days,' Johannes said, 'and I need to buy some gifts. Do you want to join me at some of the other markets?'

'Yeah sure. Do you know where they are?'

'I've got a rough idea, and a map.'

'Okay, let's go.'

They headed off in the direction of the Lal Chowk market, through back streets so narrow that shop owners could pour cups of tea from one shop to their neighbour in the next and the one opposite as well, tiny stalls packed with all sorts of exotic items, rungs hanging across the walkway with even more merchandise. It was exciting rubbing shoulders with shopkeepers whose forebears had been doing the same thing for centuries.

When they reached Lal Chowk, it was a slightly newer and more open marketplace than the back streets and Johannes immediately set about haggling for carvings made from walnut wood, pashmina shawls, miniature jewellery boxes and trinkets of all shapes and styles. Alexander enjoyed being with someone who was buying gifts for family members back home and wondered if he should sometimes do the same. The only thing he'd ever sent back was a gift for his mother's birthday, a piece of jewellery from Santorini. He'd just about completely lost touch in the last year, something that on this day he felt quite bad about. He decided to do something to rectify this, so he joined in with Johannes and began seriously looking for a gift for his mother.

'If I was to buy something for my mother, could you post it to her when you get home? It'd be more reliable and faster than sending it from here.'

'Yes of course, it'd be a pleasure.'

Alexander went from stall to stall and eventually chose an ornate little box, not much bigger than his hand, made from walnut wood and painted with minute flowers in each corner of the lid. He'd put a note inside it and wrap it later. It didn't cost much at all, but he was happy with his purchase.

Then he thought about his two little sisters, how he'd really neglected them. Only once or twice in the past year and a half of travels had he spoken to them on the phone, and then only very briefly. He'd never even sent them a gift, so right then, he began to look for something. He quickly found some lovely jewellery pieces which he knew they'd like, very different from anything they were likely to find in his home town. He'd put these two pieces in the box he bought for his mother.

It was the middle of the day and time for lunch, so they sat down beside one of the street-food stalls and ordered little *baqerkhani* pastries and milky sweet tea.

'It's great sitting here, isn't it?' Johannes said.

'Sure is. I love doing exactly this: sipping tea and watching the world go by.'

'So what's the plan for the rest of the day? Johannes asked.

'Have you bought all the gifts you wanted to buy?'

'I have now,' he said, holding up his final purchase, a colourful shawl.

'Well I've heard the gardens are pretty spectacular here. Do you want to see one or two?'

'Actually, I read something yesterday about a botanical garden which has just opened. I'll see if I can find it.' He rummaged through his shoulder bag, pulling out pieces of paper and clippings. 'Here it is, the Jawaharlal Nehru Memorial Botanical

Garden recently opened in memory of India's first prime minister.'

'Sounds good, and just recently opened! Where is it?'

'It says it's in the direction of the Zabarwan Mountain Range about ten kilometres out of town. We'll have to catch a bus to get there.'

An hour later they were entering the newly established botanic gardens. It was obviously new with many of the plants still quite small. There were a few larger trees however and everything was incredibly neat and tidy. They spent the entire afternoon walking around admiring the plants and the scenery of lakes and mountains.

At one point Johannes pulled out a small bag of hashish and together with a tiny sprinkling of tobacco began to roll a joint.

'Do you feel like a smoke?' he asked Alexander.

'I will never say no to a joint, thanks.'

And so they smoked together enjoying the serenity of the gardens. The afternoon then became a bit of a blur for both of them.

'Good hash man, thanks,' Alexander said repeatedly for the next two hours.

By late afternoon after much hilarious discussion and laughing at things that were totally unfunny, their minds were returning to reality. They had left the gardens deciding it might be a good idea to walk back to the hotel. Lost and not knowing where the hell they were, they decided to catch a taxi. It was a good idea because they were nowhere near where they thought they were.

Back in the comfort of their rooms they both individually crashed out. Night fell and in time Alexander woke Johannes asking if he was hungry.

'I'm famished as a matter of fact.'

'Totally got the munchies eh?' Alexander laughed.

They were soon walking around the neighbourhood searching for a place to eat. They decided on a traditional looking place with soft lighting and a welcoming atmosphere. After a few minutes of looking at the menu they decided on two dishes to share. The dishes they chose were an aromatic lamb dish, Rogan Josh, and a yoghurt, ginger and potato dish called Dum Aaloo. Together with naan, it was a feast for their tastebuds when it arrived and, complemented with herbal tea, it was the perfect way to end their day of adventure.

Johannes left as planned the following day, promising to send the gift to Alexander's family in Holland. Alexander had inserted a card with the gift saying what his new address was, Poste Restante Srinagar Kashmir and an explanation of which gift was for whom.

Alexander paid for a few more nights where he was staying and spent the next days walking around town sketching the wonderfully interesting scenes and characters he came across. He went back to the floating markets and sketched there too. In between, he'd read his new book, Nietzsche's *Beyond Good and Evil,* and of course was compelled to contemplate all that was going on in his head: confused and conflicting interpretations of Nietzsche's philosophy. What is this new philosophy anyway? He wondered. One thing Alexander *could* understand was how Nietzsche wrote that the future would bring with it a desire for mastery over the whole earth. Several countries like the USSR and America were doing it, and others would join the race, he could just sense it. He was tormented by this and so much more.

One day while he was sketching shikaras beside Nagin Lake a man approached him and asked to see his drawings. Alexander handed him his sketch-pad.

'They're very good,' the man commented. 'I'd like to buy some if you're interested.'

Alexander had never thought of selling his drawings. He usually gave them to people as gifts, hotel proprietors who were particularly nice to him, other travellers with whom he established a close connection. Once or twice he'd traded a piece of his art for a meal, but never had anyone wanted to pay money for them.

'Why would you want one of *my* drawings?' he asked.

'I am building some new houseboats here and I'd like to have some art on the walls of each of them depicting life on the lake, and I can see straight away that several of your sketches are highly suitable.'

Alexander could see an opportunity and asked: 'Then how much would you be willing to pay?'

'Come to my home later and we'll discuss the matter. You can bring more drawings if you have them.'

'Where do you live?' Alexander asked quite intrigued at the thought of doing business here in Kashmir.

'Turn around, you see the two storey house beyond the boats over there?'

'The white one you mean?'

'Yes that's the one.'

It was the biggest house beside the lake. Alexander thought this might mean that the man could be willing to pay a good price for his work.

'Come over this evening if you want, come for dinner too. Let's say around seven.'

This would give Alexander time to walk home and pick up the rest of his work.

'Seven would be fine,' he agreed.

'Here is my card. My name is Muzaffa Qasim.'

'I am Alexander Van der Sluijs. I am very pleased to meet you.'

'As am I.'

'See you tonight.'

'Until then.'

Alexander ran almost the whole distance back to his room, because he wanted to enhance some of his recent works so as to make them more attractive, little added strokes here and there, an improved shadow line, a bird in a tree, whatever it took. He sorted his work into three piles, not good enough or the wrong subjects and therefore unsuitable, the maybe pile and the best ones. At the end of his sorting, he felt he had several dozen appropriate drawings to present to Mr Qasim that evening.

He showered, put on his best shirt, tied his hair back and set off to meet with his potential customer. Arriving at the front door a few minutes past the hour, he rang the doorbell and was welcomed by a woman in a sari.

'Mrs Qasim?' Alexander inquired.

'No, I am maid,' she replied. 'Please to follow.'

Alexander followed the maid into a large reception room, with ornate furniture, large framed paintings, sumptuous curtains and thick hand-made carpets.

'Please to sit,' the young woman offered, and walked off.

A moment later another woman arrived.

'Mrs Qasim?' Alexander asked again, standing.

'No, I be cook,' she answered politely with a big smile, happy to have been confused with the lady of the house. Just then Mr Qasim entered the room.

'Alexander, welcome.'

'Thank you Mr Qasim.'

He directed the cook to bring some cold tea. Then they sat drinking and looking through the drawings that Alexander had brought with him.

'These are very fine drawings. I would be happy to purchase many of these.'

'May I ask if you'd like to see my other work, drawings I've done before coming to Kashmir?'

"Yes I would like to see them but not to buy. The ones I am anticipating to purchase are just for the houseboats, and only lake scenes and similar interest me.'

'Why are you interested in my work and not that of some local artist?' Alexander asked.

'Because I want something not normally seen, a fresh style,

and you have this … a fresh style. Your work captures something a little different from what we're used to. It is really very good, very refreshing. There is often too much colour in Kashmiri art.'

Just then Mrs Qasim came in. 'Come here Chandri, meet Alexander our artist.'

'Hello Alexander,' she offered with a beautifully genuine smile.

'Mrs Qasim, I'm happy to meet you.'

'So you are the artist who will adorn our new houseboats, yes?'

'I think so,' Alexander replied.

'Most definitely Chandri, here look at why,' Mr Qasim said.

They each looked through the drawings and continually demonstrated their approval in soft Kashmiri whispers to each other.

'What offer do you want to make this young artist?' Mrs Qasim asked.

'I think for twenty-five drawings, $500 in American currency, what do you think Alexander?'

He thought long before answering. 'Can I reserve my answer for a few minutes?'

'Certainly, let's have dinner, and we'll talk about other possibilities as well,' Mr Qasim announced.

He was ushered into the dining room where many dishes were being brought out by the cook and her assistant. Over dinner, the Qasims put forward a suggestion for Alexander, not only to provide five drawings each for the five soon-to-be-launched houseboats, but also a major work in colour above the bed in each houseboat's master cabin.

'Again, we'd like a lake scene or similar, would you agree to that?' Mr Qasim asked.

'Certainly,' agreed Alexander.

And so within a few days he had begun work, moving into a cottage in the garden and living right beside the lake for the time being. He had the use of a bicycle to get to the markets and had a small kitchen so that he could prepare his own meals. Regularly however, one of the maids would arrive with a steaming dish of something delicious and Alexander would need to do no cooking that night. With his job, he could work his own hours, but generally put in about seven or eight hours each day.

He visited the post office and picked up his mail. A letter from his mother thanked him for the wonderful gift, but voiced her disappointment at not having heard from him for so long. In the letter was a drawing from one of his little sisters. It revealed to him that her skill was developing. At just 9 years of age, she had drawn a picture of the canals of Amsterdam, featuring, he had to laugh, houseboats. It was a lovely drawing, coloured in with fine pencils and rather delicate toning, not what would be expected from a 9-year-old. He immediately wrote back, purchasing one of the few postcards he'd bought in the entire trip. He filled them in briefly on some news, and thanked his sister for the gift. He made a mental note not to forget to write again soon.

Occasionally Mrs Qasim would wander down to where Alexander was working to see the progress of his work. One day, she brought some tea with her and made him stop and have a break. She wanted to talk.

'Alexander,' she began, 'you seem like a highly intelligent person, how old are you?'

'I'm 21, why?'

'I was thinking, is travel the right direction in life at your age? Isn't it a waste?'

'Not at all. I'm learning more by travelling the world than I could possibly learn at university and that, most likely, would be what I'd be doing otherwise. What I'm experiencing is broader than many people can imagine. At university I wouldn't be learning anywhere near as much as I do when travelling, I'm sure of that. And I carry with me the most wonderful books. I'm learning all the time.'

'Perhaps you're right,' Mrs Qasim admitted. 'We're a bit

insular here. I sometimes forget there's a world out there, even though our customers are mostly from abroad. You see I've always loved it here. I've only ever travelled as far as India, nowhere else. Growing up here in Srinagar was very special. We didn't need to go away. Each season was unique. In spring, we'd take a break from school after our long winter. The ice and snows would melt and the fragrance of the flowers would entice us all to go outside. We would swim in the lakes and play games until late in the evening. Then slowly autumn would arrive turning the whole countryside to gold.'

'It sounds very special,' Alexander said.

'It was. We were always taught that Srinagar was a land of prosperity, and a land of peace and compassion.'

'Peace and compassion,' Alexander repeated, 'how lovely.'

After six weeks all five houseboats were finished, Alexander's paintings being the final stage before the official launch. It was an extravagant affair with friends and business associates of the Qasims, workers and dignitaries all invited to be a part of the big day.

The Qasims' fleet of houseboats was now nine, the five new ones being larger and more luxurious by far than the original ones. Now they would be able to offer customers a wider range of options. They looked magnificent all tied up alongside the jetties at the end of the lawn.

Alexander received considerable congratulations for his drawings, now all framed in beautifully varnished walnut-wood frames. He was extremely happy to have had this opportunity and asked one of the photographers if he could possibly have some of the photos when they were printed. He'd send them home to his family.

No other work offers came up even though he'd hoped they would, and so a few days later, Alexander began to think of moving on. The Qasims said he could stay in the cottage as long as he wanted so he took advantage of the offer and stayed one more week.

Now with an extra $800 in his pocket, an extraordinary amount to be paid for his work, Alexander felt confident that he could travel almost indefinitely. He'd left Amsterdam two years earlier with 2,500 guilders, nearly half of which he still had in traveller's cheques. Adding 800 US dollars, he knew he was one of the fortunate Westerners travelling the hippie trail.

Remembering a conversation he'd had with Johannes about Afghanistan, Alexander thought he might make this his next destination, so he bought a ticket to Kabul and was on his way after a few more days. The Qasims said they'd welcome him back any time he returned to Kashmir. 'Come back and have a houseboat holiday and pay nothing,' they'd said.

The journey to Kabul was quite eventful with several breakdowns in the old bus. Each time however, the driver and a skilful passenger got the engine going again and Alexander enjoyed immensely the scenery of high altitude deserts, nomads on camels and locals on foot with no apparent village or even dwelling anywhere in sight. Where do these people live, he often wondered when he saw them trudging along the highway, though a highway, it was definitely not.

After a trip that should have taken a day, but took twice that long, they rolled into Kabul a few weeks before Christmas. It was bitterly cold and Alexander thought it'd be a tough place to spend any length of time. He ended up in a boarding house with a lot of other young travellers and an abundance of hashish available for next to nothing. In fact there was so much around, he didn't need to purchase any. Instead he bought some warmer clothes including a Posteen jacket made from goatskin and swapped a drawing for a pair of warm boots which another traveller didn't need any more as he was leaving for somewhere warmer. The jacket would take up a lot of room in his rucksack if he wasn't wearing it, but it was a necessity in these temperatures. A growing number of sketch-pads was fast becoming the dominant feature to his luggage. Fortunately he'd just sold a good number of them.

Christmas was bizarre in the Kabul of 1969. Alexander and his new friends would meet in chai shops on Chicken Street and elsewhere, some smoking opium, others hashish or marijuana and newcomers would be shocked at the amount of weapons freely displayed on the belts or over the shoulders of nearly every man in town: rusty old pistols, swords, daggers ... and they certainly looked like they'd be happy to use them if needed.

Alexander was able to find some good reading from fellow travellers and swapped several of the books he'd been reading until recently while he was painting the houseboats in Srinagar. A very talented guitarist was one memorable fellow, an Aussie who, apart from having great reading material, also played guitar. His sublime and gentle plucking were softer than any guitar Alexander had ever heard played. His rich deep voice blended perfectly with the amazing notes he got out of the instrument. He told Alexander one day that his hand seemed to have a mind of its own. His brain didn't tell it what to play. His hand instead experimented and found new and surprising notes all the time.

Now, the two having met, Alexander had works by Dostoyevsky, Rousseau and Jean-Paul Sartre and spent the next weeks warming himself by various fires, his reading being interrupted only on occasion to take a puff from a hookah. The books, he felt, were far better than the hashish or opium, even though the drugs were amongst the finest in the world.

The day before the start of a new decade, a few friends got together and invited Alexander for a picnic outside Kabul in the village of Istalif, a centuries-old centre for pottery. It was about a 25 kilometre journey and five of them hired a private taxi to get them there. It was a joyous occasion, all of these young travellers keen to explore the culture of Afghanistan rather than the drug scene. Alexander discovered that all four of his fellow picnickers were studying in their various countries and had taken a year off to travel the hippie trail. There was a girl from England studying law, a young Russian fellow about to finish a physics degree, and two Australians studying medicine. All of them were keen to talk about life and love, travel and mankind, history, war and other subjects while sitting overlooking the town and enjoying a picnic which the English girl had prepared. Not one joint was rolled the whole day, and Alexander found the discussions quite refreshing.

Towards the end of their meal, the two Australian medical students began to discuss a book they had both just finished reading, Dostoyevsky's *The Brothers Karamazov*. It became an intense discussion. Both these guys, Paul and his friend Andy, got into a rather heated debate as to who of the four brothers deserved the reader's sympathy most. Fortunately they didn't come to blows, but Alexander discovered that Aussies definitely don't hold back with their opinions.

Throughout the hours that followed, they discussed a lot of subjects including, after the two Australians had settled down, the teachings of Sai Baba who, Alexander learned from Paul, cared little for possessions as others did, his sole concern being the realisation of the self.

'He gave equal time to the religions of both Hinduism and Islam,' Paul told them, 'and many of his devotees can't agree on which is the more important to him.'

'Have you studied his work?' Alexander asked.

'I have, yes.'

'Are you yourself a follower?' asked Sophie, the English girl.

'No,' answered Paul, 'just a student of much of the philosophical writings and thoughts which emanate from India. I remember hearing recently that one of Sai Baba's most well-known aphorisms is *Sabka Malik Ek*: One God governs all. And I like to think that as time goes on, more people will come to the realisation that this has to be the case. Give God any name, call him or her what you want, but know that if there is a supreme being, there can only be one. All Gods are one, he says. There is no difference between Hindu and Muslim. Mosque and temple are the same.'

Sophie then began to speak. 'I'm reading a book by Sri Anandamayi Ma. She was born in Bangladesh where I have just come from. She feels that a devotion to each other is of equal importance to a devotion to any God. Life and religion are one, she advises. All that you do to maintain your life, your everyday work and play, all your attempts to earn a living, should be done with sincerity, love and devotion, with a firm conviction that true living means virtually perfecting one's spiritual existence in tune with the universe. To bring about this synthesis, religious culture should be made as natural and easy as taking our food and drink when we are hungry and thirsty.'

'May I have a loan of that book after you finish it?' inquired Alexander.

'Sure, no problem,' offered Sophie. 'What do you like to read?'

'Anything that gets my thoughts flowing, but Krishnamurti and Hesse are my favourites at the moment.'

'I too like these authors,' started Andrei from Russia.

'I'm very into Krishnamurti,' added Andy.

'I have some of the works of Swami Sivananda,' continued Andrei. 'You might like to have a loan of these too.'

'I've not heard that name,' stated Alexander.

Andrei looked through his shoulder bag and pulled from it a book. Flipping through the pages he began, '*You are the master of your destiny.*' Turning pages, he added, '*A mountain is composed of tiny grains of earth. The ocean is made up of tiny drops of water. Even so, life is not an endless series of little details, actions, speeches, and thoughts. And the consequences whether good or bad of even the least of them are far-reaching.'*

'I like the sound of that,' said Alexander. 'The words, "you are the master of your destiny", I do know from somewhere.'

Andrei continued, *'Cultivate peace first in the garden of your heart by removing the weeds of lust, hatred, greed, selfishness and jealousy. Then only you can manifest it externally. Then only those who come in contact with you will be benefited by your vibrations of peace and harmony. The Divine within you is stronger than anything that is without you. Therefore be not afraid of anything. Rely on your own inner self, the divinity within you. Tap the source through looking within. Improve yourself. Build your character. Purify the heart. Develop the divine virtues. Eradicate evil traits. Conquer all that is base in you. Endeavour to attain all that is worthy and noble. Make the lower nature the servant of the higher through discipline, Tapas, self-restraint and meditation. This is the beginning of your freedom.'*

This eclectic group of travellers knew a fair bit about freedom already, and this is where the discussion headed for the next hour. Alexander prompted lively dialogue with his comments, 'All the things which remind us of being free, the gentle wind on our face, the fresh air of the mountains, the sound of crashing waves at the seaside, the songs of nature's animal world, the reading of good books, all are events in our lives which we should not only cherish and share with others but strive to make more commonplace for all.'

The driver whom they had hired in the morning to take them out here had stayed around and visited friends in Istalif for the day and was there to drive them back as planned after dark. It had been a very different day and a unique way to finish the 1960s although what was planned for the night was quite unusual too.

On the way back to Kabul, Paul and Andy suggested that they all go to the Kabul Golf Club to bring in the New Year and the new decade as they'd heard there were to be several well-known Afghani musicians playing until the early hours. It ended up being an astonishing night of music and dance. At midnight the large crowd counted down from ten to one and Alexander was approached by Sophie, for a kiss. Meaningfully and whispering in Alexander's ear she said, 'Farewell to the 60s, the decade in which we all grew up.'

The 70s had begun.

CHAPTER FOUR

The first of January 1970 was just like any other day in Kabul. Afghanistan's New Year isn't until late March, but for the Westerners residing in the country, it was a continuation of the night before. It was the dawn of a new decade, the swinging 60s had gone.

Alexander and his new friends sought to continue on from the previous day. Their other friends soon considered them somewhat of a breakaway group when every time they asked them to join in for a smoke, they declined. It wasn't that they didn't want to get stoned. It's just that they didn't want to do it so often and after the healthy philosophical discussions from the previous day, they were keen to continue their conversation.

They met at their favourite chai shop on Chicken Street, each pulled up a stool beside the window, ordered drinks and got stuck into a healthy chinwag on why the human race is so eager to be at war. Others joined in and it soon became a typical hippie discussion, half those involved being intelligent and having good points worth mentioning and half being off their faces on one drug or another. It wasn't quite what the group had planned but it was certainly interesting and acted as a catalyst for further discussions over the weeks that followed. The group increased in size and all manner of people joined in at various times and at various venues, sometimes chai shops, other times at boarding houses and restaurants. It became an even more eclectic group from tremendously diverse backgrounds and from many countries. Alexander was by no means the youngest. There were several people younger than him and the oldest was in his fifties. The subject matter was wide-ranging and became even more so as time went on. One day they discussed Aldous Huxley's *Brave New World.*

'I always thought that Huxley's ideas on drugs were quite spot-on,' Alexander announced to the group, just to see where the conversation would head. It appeared from the discussion that followed that this was the general consensus.

Mostly the group discussed literature and philosophy, and Alexander was pleased to have been so well-read. He didn't always add his two bobs' worth, remembering his high school teacher's words: 'We have two ears and one mouth. We should go through life using them in that proportion.'

People came through Kabul for all lengths of time: weeks, months and even years. It looked to Alexander like some had been around for a long time when he saw the drugged-out layabouts all around the city. Very few travellers stayed just a few days. Kabul and in fact the entire country at the time was a very charming place, but an addictive one, making it hard to leave for some.

Places worth a visit were many, and everyone it seemed had their own favourite. Those too stoned missed out. Alexander felt that a visit to the Khanqah-Shah-i-Hamadam Mosque was a highlight. Built with no visible nails, the 1730's building stands on the site of the original mosque built hundreds of years earlier by a Persian saint whose entourage most likely introduced Kashmiris to the art of carpet-making.

After a couple of months, Alexander himself felt it was time to move on, but one final journey out of Kabul was on his agenda prior to leaving. He'd heard of the magnificent countryside around Band-e Amir Lake to the west of the city, so one day he caught a bus out there with his sketch-pad and drew several views of the lake from different vantage points. It was a sunny day fortunately and the blue of the lake was similar to the blue of the Mediterranean, he thought.

But it was time to move on. Alexander thought about the route he might take and in the end decided upon more of the same: the one-step-at-a-time approach. The majority of travellers doing the hippie trail, as it was fast becoming known, came from Europe and wound up in India or Southeast Asia. Alexander though was doing his journey the other way round, and diverting off it all the time.

On a particularly cold morning, Alexander boarded a bus out of Kabul and headed off for his next destination, Kandahar, founded by Alexander the Great in 329 BC. He wanted to get there just for this fact and, when he arrived, he stayed only a few days shacking up in yet another cheap boarding house but this time sticking to himself. He visited various mosques and shrines and spent an afternoon at the market, the Herat Bazaar, sketching.

After three days Alexander moved on again, this time to Herat, situated in a fertile valley on the Hari River, and once referred to as the bread basket of Central Asia. Here he fell terribly ill for the first time since India where he had suffered from amoebic dysentery. Back then, his condition had worsened progressively over the days until he found help because he hadn't known how to treat his problem. Here it was just Delhi belly. Something he'd eaten the day before was probably the cause, but it could have been the water. So many people in his travels had told him horrifying stories of illnesses suffered in places where it was difficult to find a doctor who could speak anything other than the local language, but he knew to keep hydrated and to add some potassium salts to his diet. Slowly over the next two days, his state improved but he still was in bed most of the time, the only journey away being to the toilet. He was glad to have brought up the subject with the two Australian medical students in Kabul one day. They had offered advice for the future if ever such a problem arose which consisted of drinking plenty of clean water, adding potassium and carrying an appropriate antibiotic that was to be taken after a self-diagnosis. They had even given him a packet of weird-looking pills and he immediately began to take them upon arrival in Herat. Two days later he was almost well enough to venture outside, but he went no further than the roof-top terrace for a bit of sun. The following day he could manage a walk around town and by day four he was back to his old self.

Herat was a small city, smaller than both Kabul and Kandahar, and Alexander, now that his health was better, liked the place. It was easier to get around by public transport and the weather was now warming up. The fact that the occasional spring day arrived soothed his senses. The temperature even reached double figures sometimes. He was restless though and didn't know exactly why. He'd been in Asia for more than two years by this time and although he'd met some fascinating characters and immersed himself in exotic cultures, he felt a bit lonely and lost. He'd only had a couple of periods of romance in all those twenty odd months, and felt he'd really like to be sharing this adventure with someone who he didn't have to say goodbye to every time he moved on, someone who'd stick with him, share the decision-making and also someone to cuddle up to in a genuine and loving relationship. It'll happen, he decided, if and when it's meant to.

After his health improved, Alexander stayed in Herat for almost a week. He moved on to Islam Qala on the border with Iran and then to Dogharoon. Islam Qalam was a flat and desolate exit post. Alexander had to wait for a connecting bus. He didn't know that he had to walk to Dogharoon in order to catch it, so he wasted an hour sitting in the sun before he found out. At least he was warm.

CHAPTER FiVE

Walking over in no man's land between the two countries, an old beaten up Peugeot pulled up beside him. 'After border,' the driver started, 'you want lift?'

As the driver looked reasonably safe, Alexander thought he might give this new mode of transport a go. 'Yes okay, thanks.'

A short time later as Alexander and the driver had passed through passport control, he got into the car and they rattled off down the road together.

'Where you from?' The driver asked.

'From Holland,' Alexander replied.

'Why you call Holland and not Netherland?'

'The correct name is the Netherlands. It refers to the whole country. Holland refers to just a small part. I use the term Holland when I'm away from my home, because most people understand this. At home, I call it Nederland.'

'Thank you, I always was wonder.'

'What's your name?' Alexander inquired.

'I am Boris,' the man replied, 'and you?'

'I'm Alexander.'

'Alexander from Nederland. Good. Alexander and Boris travel Iran, sound good, make film ... Alexander and Boris, I like.'

Alexander wondered if he should have got in the car with this man, but he seemed harmless enough. He was very big with a bushy moustache, unshaven in old clothes and smelt like he hadn't showered for some time. But he was jovial enough, and Alexander settled in for the drive.

'How far are you going?' he asked.

'Today I drive to my home Bojnurd, very nice city, you like.'

'How far?'

'Some hours, afternoon we arrive.'

'Is it on the way to Tehran?' Alexander asked, worried that he might be getting taken off the highway at some stage.

'Yes, about half to finish, half distance, you understand?'

'Yeah,' he replied.

'You smoke hashish?' Boris asked.

'Sometimes.'

'You pack chillum?' Boris asked as he pulled out a bag of hash, marijuana and a chillum.

'Okay,' Alexander smiled.

A few minutes later they were sharing a chillum and bonding.

'I buy from Kandahar,' he admitted. 'I go often, car has many kilos.'

Alexander immediately freaked out, wondering if this was a safe thing to be doing, travelling with a drug dealer in Iran.

'You no worry. I know police. I pay, is no problem,' he said as he puffed away and passed the chillum to Alexander, who was already quite stoned after just one hit.

The morning became quite eventful as they slowed down regularly for herds of various animals blocking the road, and even more interesting when a broken down bus blocked the highway. They stopped to help and Boris successfully got it going to the rapturous applause of everyone on board.

It turned out to be a wonderful journey. They stopped for lunch at a place where everyone seemed to know Boris and when they pulled into Bojnurd, Boris asked Alexander if he'd like to stay at his home.

'You meet wife, kids, we eat.'

Alexander was certainly up for it so he agreed and, after a few minutes' drive through the streets, they arrived at a compound which, although it appeared a bit of a fortress with its high fence and locked gates, was neat and tidy and had all the appearances of being owned by a successful person who Boris probably was.

His wife and children came out to meet them, all chattering away in Farsi. He hugged each one of them in turn.

'Yasmin, this my friend Alexander,' Boris said to his wife.

'Hello,' she said.

'Hallo,' Alexander replied.

'Yasmin speak good English, study England, economics, teach here for government.'

'Come inside Alexander, tell me about your trip.'

Little did this woman know that asking Alexander about his trip might take more time than she imagined.

'I go for shower,' Boris said.

The children were like any kids, three of them under the age of ten. They spoke no English although Yasmin told him that the oldest had just started to study English at school.

'It's a lovely home you have,' Alexander told her.

'We are lucky. Our government looks after teachers. And I am even more fortunate. Our Shah, Mohammed Reza Shah Pahlavi, fosters economic growth and maintains a pro-Western foreign policy. For those, like me, who teach economics, we are offered many benefits. Life is good here. It is a very safe place to bring up children. They go to good schools and have excellent teachers.'

'How long did you study in England?' Alexander asked.

'I was there for three years at university and did my master's degree back here, but in Tehran, not here in Bojnurd, as we have no university.'

'You work for the government, did I understand that correctly?'

'We have a program for exceptionally gifted high school students to study preliminary courses after hours in several fields: medicine, economics and science. I am one of the lecturers for this group. I also assist with the government and I go once every month for a few days to Tehran to teach.'

'Now, tell me about yourself Alexander. How long have you been travelling?'

'It is now more than two and a half years, nearly three in fact.'

'And how can you afford to do this?'

'Before I left, I saved hard doing two jobs while finishing high school, then my parents and grandparents gave me some money which has lasted well. Last year I sold some drawings in Kashmir and I worked for six weeks there too, so my travel money has been topped up.'

'I am impressed. Where have you travelled?'

'I began by catching a bus from my home to Athens, visited some of the Greek Islands and then went to India and Nepal for over a year. After that I travelled to Kashmir and Afghanistan. Today my journey continues in Iran.'

'Well Alexander, let us make this part of your journey extra special.'

Just then Boris returned from upstairs, fresh and looking a lot different from before. 'So you get know my wife?'

'Yes Boris, we've been discussing our study and travel.'

'You have also studied Alexander?'

'My learning is from my journeys.'

'The university of life,' Yasmin stated.

'I've never thought of my travels like that.'

'But you have learned more, I think, than many formal courses of education, is this right?' She asked.

'Oh yes, when I look back to the many people I have met, the many villages, towns, cities, rivers, mountains, deserts, the conversations I have had in these diverse places, I just know that my path of learning is a unique one. And the right one for me.'

'Alexander likes to draw Boris,' Yasmin told him.

'What you draw?' Boris asked interested.

'I like to sketch scenery mostly, but in my travels, I have drawn many things: people, animals, lots of subjects.'

'Can we see some later?' Yasmin asked.

'Sure.'

'Dinner first though,' she added. She called the children who politely sat around the table and Alexander remembered a similar scene of domesticity when his mother called him and his sisters to dinner. Unlike this family dinner table however, his was more unruly.

The meal was a very good one. After so much travel where Alexander found himself in cheap restaurants and taking a punt at dubious street stalls, this was a welcome change. He hadn't eaten so well since being with the Qasims in Srinagar.

After dinner, he brought out his several sketch-pads and impressed his hosts no end. The children weren't interested so they went off to another room.

'When you return to the Netherlands,' started Yasmin, 'you'll be able to have an art show. All of these show extraordinary talent.'

'Thank you, but I don't plan to go home for some time. Maybe never.'

'Why is that?' Yasmin asked curiously. 'What have you done?'

'Well, I left because I didn't want to go into the army.'

'Here in Iran, this not possible,' Boris stated emphatically.

'What my husband means is that it is not possible to relinquish one's duties to do military service, it is simply illegal, punishable by prison.'

'It's not much different where I come from.'

'Yes but you can do alternative service,' Yasmin said.

'Why you no do this?' added Boris.

'I had no desire to have anything to do with fighting, whether it meant holding a gun, or doing what my country considered an alternative. I felt it was just plain wrong.'

'Many people here would not understand these sentiments. Having lived in the UK though, I know that this is how many Europeans feel. And with the Vietnam War, Americans and

Australians are objecting too. But it is vastly different here.'

'How so?' asked Alexander.

'You see,' Yasmin continued, 'at the moment our government policy on the military is to upgrade and renew. The Shah wants to expand our military, buy new weapons, tanks, fighter planes. Our economy is booming. Oil prices are rising. The idea is to have a strong and professional army, navy and air force capable of protecting our interests here in the Middle East, and most of the population are in agreement.'

'Yasmin we have no navy to speak of,' Boris interrupted.

'But darling it is planned to renew the ships and make our navy stronger than ever before.'

'The years ahead might not be, how you say in English, smooth sailing,' Boris added, not realising the pun.

'I think enough said,' Yasmin declared, 'who's ready for desert?'

She left the room, calling the children back and returned with some *Zulbia* and *Sohan Gazi*, both totally new to Alexander and extremely delicious.

'Tomorrow, Alexander, I would like to take you to one of my classes. It is a short one, so although you won't understand much, it will give you a chance to visit the school, to meet some students, and of course for them to meet you, and perhaps to see some of our facilities, like the library. Do you like to read?'

'I love to read,' he admitted.

'What subjects do you like?'

'Philosophy mainly.'

'Do you have any favourite authors?'

'Hesse, Krishnamurti, Dostoyevsky, Jean-Paul Sartre and others,' Alexander replied proudly.

'Oh my God, you are well-read. Yes you must come, but I think the library you should visit is in our capital. We have books in many languages, but mainly of course in Farsi, but English as well. I don't know about Dutch. Tell me do you read in English?'

'I read Hesse in German, but most other books in English.'

'So you speak German, English and Dutch.'

'Correct.'

'Any others?'

'No, but I always try to learn a few words upon entering a new country.'

'What words? Boris asked highly interested.

'*Please* and *thank you* first, then *how much* and *too much*.'

They all laughed.

'*Where* and *when* are more important than *why* and *how*, but slowly you pick up words even when you don't try. In Greece I tried hard because it was the beginning of my travels, and I liked the language very much. Also the Greek people are happy always to teach you a few words, all the people. In India, most people speak English, and I think it is the most beautiful English spoken anywhere. In Kashmir, greetings were important, the same in Afghanistan. Here, I don't know yet.'

'Well for your first night please is *lotfan* and thank you is *mamnoon*.' This is Farsi, same as Afghanistan.

'Lotfan, may I use the toilet?'

Again they all laughed.

'Come I show where,' Boris offered.

On the way, Boris showed him the guest room and said he could have a shower if he would like.

'I would very much like, *mamnoon* Boris.'

Alexander felt he'd really fallen on his feet here, a welcoming family with kids who weren't demanding and didn't get in the way, an invitation to a school the following day and at last a decent meal and a shower.

He slept like a baby when he climbed into bed.

The visit to the school the following day was a real eye-opener. He didn't expect all the students to be so interested in him, nor to be so well-dressed and keen to practise their English. Little economics was learned but the students sure as hell learned a lot about a young Westerner travelling the world.

He stayed with the family another night and then farewelled them. They drove him to the bus station and he bought a ticket to Tehran. As a gift, he presented them with two of his drawings, and both Yasmin and Boris were overjoyed.

Tehran was hectic. A city of many millions. Alexander thought he'd stay just a little while and then definitely get out. It was now June, three years since he started his trip. Tehran was at its hottest from June to August. He went to the library as was suggested by Yasmin, saw the beginning stages of the Azadi Tower being built to commemorate 2500 years of the Persian Empire, and then left for Baghdad travelling by train for a change. The temperature was unbearable when he disembarked. He didn't want to get an air-conditioned room due to the exorbitant cost but for a Dutchman temperatures in the mid-forties were simply too much to handle so he did.

While in the hotel, he met an Iranian entrepreneur who offered him a job driving cars back and forth between Baghdad and Tehran. He wasn't desperate for cash, but Alexander thought he'd better do it. Opportunities to earn some money don't present themselves every day.

'Are they air-conditioned?' he asked hoping the cars would be.

'Some are,' he was told.

'How much do I get paid?'

'Between one and two hundred American dollars each trip.'

'Each direction?'

'Yes of course. And we drive in convoy, so getting through the border is my concern.'

So that's what he did all through the summer, occasionally being lucky enough to have air-conditioning, but when there was none, he just hoped he could drive fast enough for a successful air-flow through the open windows. Getting across the border was totally dodgy, but his boss got him through by paying the border guards bribes and rarely was there any problem, either at the border or anywhere else for that matter.

By the end of the summer, he'd been able to save nearly 3,000 dollars, all expenses being paid whilst en route each and every time. He did the round trip ten times and his boss said that few others over the years had been able to maintain the speed as well as he had.

He often thought to himself how fortunate he was to have arrived during the hottest days of summer. Otherwise, he wouldn't have booked into an air-conditioned hotel, and would surely not have met the car dealer. At the end of his stint though he was happy to move on. The daily temperature was rarely over forty anymore, but it was often in the mid to high thirties.

CHAPTER SiX

From Baghdad he travelled west across the Syrian Desert in the direction of Israel. He wanted to stop travelling so much for a while and thought that a period on an Israeli kibbutz would be rewarding. He liked the communal idea of living off the land and as he knew little about farming thought it was time to learn.

He discovered that kibbutz life began in the early years of the twentieth century and only twenty years before his arrival, 7.5 percent of the population lived on a kibbutz. Now in 1970, that had increased somewhat with 12,000 foreigners arriving each year and joining the locals. They lived by the Marxist principle: from each according to his ability, to each according to his needs.

Alexander wound up at a kibbutz called Beit Guvrin where there were about a hundred people living and working, twenty or so being from other countries. Again Alexander found himself regularly absorbed in philosophical discussions as most of those working on kibbutzim from abroad were students on various journeys of discovery. After three years on the road, this was a relaxing respite even though he had to work six hours a day, six days a week.

With money in his pocket, he didn't need to earn much, and anyway the workers only received pocket money for their efforts as their accommodation and food was provided. And of course there's no price you can put on the knowledge that was gained by these workers from other lands.

They picked apples mainly, at first anyway, but eventually they harvested crops and planted seeds to bring on the second round of such vegetables as lettuce, celery, spinach, watermelon, rockmelon and countless herbs were harvested and planted continuously.

A week or so after Alexander began on the kibbutz, a girl from New Zealand joined the work force and he could tell that she immediately took a liking to him. She was very attractive with jet black hair and unusual green eyes. She could pick apples almost as fast as Alexander from day one. It had taken him a whole week to reach this speed. And she could carry a fair load to the tractor too. On the first evening after they'd finished work and were waiting in the dining hall for dinner, he felt he had to compliment her on the speed she maintained and the number of kilos she picked.

'You're pretty fast you know,' he started, 'aren't you tired?'

'No I'm used to this work. My parents grow apples in New Zealand.'

'Ah so you're from New Zealand.'

'Yes, and you?' she asked.

'Holland, the Netherlands,' he replied. 'What's your name?'

'Fiona, but my friends call me Fi.'

'I'm Alexander and almost nobody calls me Alex.'

'Can I?'

'Sure you can,' Alexander replied emphatically. The name Alexander was always a bit of a mouthful he felt.

'So what's the deal here, Alex?'

'What with the food you mean?'

'Yeah.'

'Well by about six, they'll have a buffet laid out and you can choose what you want. It's quite good, with the choice as well as the quality.'

'I'm looking forward to this. I haven't eaten properly in weeks.'

'Why's that?'

'Travelling up the east coast of Africa, it's been a bit tough on the system.'

'How do you mean, bad stomach?'

'Yes and the rest, plus it's just hard to get anything decent and safe in some places. Add to that getting sick and it's all a bit hard.'

'You'll be able to get back on track here I think,' Alex said.

'Hope so,' Fiona replied.

The food started to be brought out and displayed as it was every evening around this time, and soon people started casually helping themselves to what was on offer. There was plenty for everyone.

After dinner Fiona asked, 'Hey Alex do you feel like a walk?'

There was a new moon in the western sky and as the sun had not long gone down, there was still plenty of light. 'Sure,' he said. He wanted to ask her about Africa, so this was his chance. They walked around the compound checking it all out.

'I'm glad I decided to come here, Alex. Africa was good, but I needed a break.'

'How long were you there?'

'Six months. I planned on longer, but maybe some other time.'

'So how did you start? Where did you come from?'

'I flew in from Perth to Joburg, seven months ago roughly, travelled north via Rhodesia and Malawi and eventually up the coast to Addis Ababa in Ethiopia and then just had to get out.'

'So you came here.'

'Yeah there were cheapish flights from Addis to Jerusalem, and as I'd always wanted to work on a kibbutz I thought it was the right time.'

'How did you choose this kibbutz?'

'I saw a note on the notice board where I stayed in Jerusalem and phoned them here. They said that they needed people continuously and sounded friendly, so I bought a bus ticket and came. They said they'd trial me for a few days, and so far I like it.'

'I'm sure they'll keep you because you work well. It's all about the numbers. You probably picked more apples today than I did. I'd better be careful not to lose my own job,' Alex said although he wasn't really worried.

'You said you had to get out when you were in Ethiopia, why?'

'The people are so poor, the drought means they have no food. Some make it to the city and just live on the streets begging. It's not very nice.'

'It's a bit like that in India too,' Alex admitted. 'Not everywhere but in some places it is.'

'Okay, your turn, tell me about your trip.'

'I started three years ago ...'

'Three years,' Fiona interrupted, a bit taken aback.

'Yeah, caught a bus from Amsterdam to Athens, caught various ferries to some of the islands, then flew to New Delhi and travelled around India and Nepal for over a year.'

'Boy, you've really done your journey thoroughly then.'

'Uhuh, but then to Kashmir where I worked for while ...'

'Doing what?'

'Painting.'

'What, houses?'

'No houseboats, but not that sort of painting. I draw and sketch and a couple who were building a small fleet of houseboats wanted a large painting inside each of them, and asked if I'd care to do the paintings. They also bought a lot of my drawings and framed them. It was a good few months.'

'Fantastic.'

'Yeah it was pretty good. They even let me stay beside the lake in their garden cottage.'

'That sounds perfect, Alex.'

'After that I went to Kabul in Afghanistan, and finally Iran before coming here.'

'So in three years you've only worked once?'

'No, I spent a whole summer driving back and forth from Baghdad to Tehran delivering and picking up cars.'

'Cars, what was that all about?'

'I met this car dealer and he needed cars moved around. He

was a bit dodgy. He had to pay the border police, but I was up for it. It was just cars.'

'Yeah but the boot might have had drugs hidden somewhere,' Fiona said with a worried look on her face.

'I don't think so.'

'But you're not sure, are you?'

'Not a hundred percent, no.'

'Wow, you were game. I certainly wouldn't have done it. But three years on the road. That's totally impressive.'

'So what are your plans after Israel?'

'I dunno,' Fiona admitted. 'What about you?'

'Africa, I think, but I've got no idea where. It's a big continent. I'll just talk with people who I meet, like you. I've got to find out more about the places you've been to.'

'Yeah I'd like that.'

In the weeks that followed Fiona and Alex became a team. They worked picking apples nearly every day, spoke about their respective travels, discussed their desires, their fears, their backgrounds. Alex discovered that Fiona had studied an arts course at university but told her that he could never decide what to study so he just read what he considered to be important literature and travelled. He sketched Fiona often while they had their talks, and she was more than impressed with the results.

'I've never had someone sketch or draw me,' she said after the first one was finished. 'It really looks like me.'

'Yeah of course, that's the point.'

'I know that, but you're really good, really, really good.'

After he'd done a few more, he made her pick her favourite, and together with a small bunch of flowers gave it to her one evening.

'I'll keep it forever, thank you so much,' she said and gave him a little kiss.

A month or so after Fiona's arrival on one of their days off, Alex invited her to the Sidonian Burial Caves in the nearby Beit

Guvrin National Park. He'd heard a lot about them and wanted to go exploring.

They were told by the manager of the kibbutz that if they looked hard enough they'd probably find some old artefacts, and sure enough they did: little lamps, cracked bowls, pieces of pottery. Although a certain amount of archaeological excavation had taken place early in the century, it'd be another twenty years before proper excavation would be carried out.

They visited many of the underground rooms. There were literally hundreds of them, many interconnected through a series of underground tunnels. Some of the caves were certainly more than just caves, which is not what they expected. They sat alone in a number of them and just talked. A few were even painted and were more like chapels.

'It's a great place for contemplation down here,' Alex began.

'I love it, thanks for bringing me here.'

'You're welcome,' he replied. 'It feels like the worries of the world disappear down here, don't you think?' Alex asked.

'Yeah a bit,' Fiona answered.' If we humans stopped to think a little, the world could so easily be a better place.'

'How do you mean?' asked Alex.

'Well, the world of the twentieth century is mad and it's getting madder, don't you agree?'

'Oh yeah it's mad alright.'

'I reckon it's dark and getting darker, out of whack and getting wackier.'

'I wouldn't disagree with that.'

'Apart from mother-nature, some of the rivers, mountains, perhaps the oceans and the water cycle, everything else is out of kilter,' she continued. 'Sometimes it's not out by very much. Ten percent maybe. I've got a theory. It's strange but imagine this: If 10 percent of employed people decided to job share, or 10 percent of workers took a 10 percent cut in their wage, unemployment would be almost non-existent, a massive problem sorted out in one easy manoeuvre.

'Taking it one step further, if every wage earner on the planet gave up 10 percent of that wage, and I mean everybody, rich and poor, big wage earners and people who earn almost nothing, and we put in all into one big pot and then redistributed it all amongst every wage earner who had originally contributed, a lot of the world's problems of hunger and the impoverished would also be solved. Just imagine a destitute Ethiopian farmer suddenly having a thousand dollars, or even a hundred. You'd probably only have to do the exercise once.'

'Interesting,' was all Alex could say.

'And consider this. If 10 percent of people who drank before driving, if 10 percent of couples planning to marry, if 10 percent of criminals considering their crime would all reconsider and do the opposite, the world would undoubtedly be a better place.'

'You're quite weird I think,' Alex stated.

'Hang on, there's more to my weird theory. While we're on the subject of marriage, if we all had a re-think, then maybe, just maybe the results of success in the matrimonial department would improve. Just think for a moment about the failure rate of marriages in the West. It's about a third these days and it'll probably be nearly half by the end of the twentieth century ... nearly half the total of people getting married won't succeed in the 'until death do us part' section of the deal. This is only a prediction, but even if it levels out at a third, imagine if a third of the planes that took off crashed, or ships sank, or car brakes failed, there'd be an absolute bloody uproar, and rightly so. Why then, do we accept such a poor set of figures for marriage? I personally reckon it's high time to have a re-think. We might even get marriage failure down to 10 percent.'

'I don't know about that,' admitted Alex.

'Nor do I. It's only a theory.'

CHAPTER SEVEN

Alex and Fiona spent more and more time together as the days went by. It was becoming inevitable that they would leave the kibbutz and travel together. Sure enough Alex popped the question four months after his arrival, three months after hers. She didn't immediately say yes, but he kept asking, and eventually she saw the sense in it.

'Where would we go though?' she asked.

'Why not Africa? You said you wanted to see more of the place, and I've wanted to go there. Most importantly though, it's pretty close. Then I could take you to the Greek Islands.'

'I dunno. I'll have to think about this. I want to travel somewhere with you, but I don't know if returning to Africa is the right choice. I only left three months ago.'

In the weeks that followed he kept trying to convince her and one day it seemed she'd made up her mind. 'I will come with you to Africa, Alex, but to places where I haven't been yet.'

'I'm so happy. Let's start making a plan,' he suggested.

They spoke with others who had spent time on the African continent and decided to enter via Egypt, go across the northern countries of Libya and Algeria and then to Morocco. If all went well, they'd proceed south into the sub Saharan countries. Otherwise they could change their minds and head to Greece.

They gave their notice to the kibbutz manager and a week later departed for Cairo. President Nasser had not long died and Anwar Sadat was making sweeping changes including a break with the Soviet Union so as to become an ally of the United States.

Alex and Fiona cared little about anything else but seeing the pyramids and moving on ever closer to Morocco, their first major destination. Weeks of arduous travel through Libya and Algeria saw them relying upon each other through very difficult times. People continuously tried to rip them off. Men did bizarre things with their eyes when looking at Fiona, the food was usually very ordinary, and although they didn't get sick, they always felt crook in the guts.

They arrived in Marrakech totally worn out and in need of a good rest. It was just before Christmas. They booked in to the Hotel Ali next to Jemaa el-Fnaa Square which was a hive of activity with buses coming and going. Years later it would become altogether different turning into a night market with traffic banned from the area. On the other side of the square was the start of the medina, the historic part of Marrakech founded by the Almoravids in 1070, and several outstanding monuments still stood from that era, such as the Kasbah and the Koutoubiya Mosque as well as some of the original gardens and battlements.

After the travel Alex and Fiona had endured in recent weeks, the room they were given was heaven. They sank into their bed and slept without waking until the next day.

Fiona woke before Alex, deciding to go quietly outside and see what was happening. She climbed to the rooftop terrace where she could see the square and the line of horse-drawn carriages opposite the entrance to the hotel. She wanted to go in one, to ride the streets of Marrakech with her new lover.

She watched the action for a few minutes, smelt the aromas of various spices not knowing which was which. Then she went back to their room. Opening the door, she disturbed Alex. 'Oh I'm glad you're awake, I've got a surprise for you.'

'What is it?'

'You'll have to wait, because it's a surprise. Come on, get ready.'

After Alex freshened up and got dressed, she dragged him excitedly downstairs and across the road to the long line of carriages. 'We're going on one of these, my shout.'

And off they went. It was beautiful, moving through Marrakech at such a slow pace taking it all in from the comfort of a horse-drawn open carriage with the warmth of early morning bathing them.

'Thank you so much Fiona. I'm loving this,' Alex cried in appreciation. First they trotted around the old walls of the medina, then from street to street and highlight to enchanting highlight. Everything was amazing, the sounds of the horse with its neighing and its hooves on the cobblestones, the classic Moroccan architecture with the intricate woodwork and huge wooden doors, the big arches, the minarets and even the traffic.

'As soon as I saw the carriages down beside the park, I knew this would be a great way to properly start our Moroccan adventure,' Fiona said.

After about an hour, the driver delivered them back to Jemaa el-Fnaa where they searched for a restaurant to eat breakfast. When they chose a place, they were brought a basket of breads and pastries with jams and sweet mint tea. Afterwards they walked through the narrow back streets of the centuries-old medina intrigued at all the trading and the delightful aromas of the many spices.

They wandered for hours around the medina and the streets beyond. In the days that followed they visited many of the magical wonders of Marrakech. Being a Muslim country, Christmas was not celebrated, but Fiona and Alex did their own thing, celebrating by themselves. Alex sketched the action around town, the snake charmers, the horse-drawn caleches, the market itself. Then the next day they caught a bus to the coast, to Essaouira which, until recently, had been known as Mogador. The port was large with substantial fishing boats returning with their catch and for centuries had been known as the safest anchorage on the Moroccan coast.

It was a windy place though and the Alize breeze blew strong most days they were there. Enormous seagulls positioned themselves all around the port so as to grab any morsel from unsuspecting visitors as well as anything thrown from the fishing boats. It was a town full of magnificent art, encouraged by sculptor Boujemaa Lakhdar who had some years earlier opened an art museum. They spent New Year here. It was now 1971.

In each of the places they'd so far visited, Marrakech and Essaouira, they'd stayed less than a week and it was the same at Agadir, their next stop. January was too cold to swim, and they had to make a decision. If they were to turn around and head for the Mediterranean, it'd be cold there too. If they headed south the weather would get warmer, but would just a few months be long enough to travel down the entire West African region? They decided it would and so made plans to head into the Sub-Saharan countries.

They were getting along well as co-travellers, had become closer to each other and appeared to be falling in love. There'd be testing times ahead though, as West Africa in the 1970s was by no means an easy or safe region to travel.

CHAPTER EiGHT

They'd heard of a train journey from Zouerate to Nouadhibou and decided to make their way by whatever method they could to get to Sub-Saharan Mauritania. They hitch-hiked, caught inexpensive taxis, walked in the desert, bribed officials at check points and both agreed that at the end of it, they'd just experienced the toughest week of their lives. Little did they know at the time, that things were going to get decidedly more difficult.

They spent a night getting cleaned up in Zouerate and next day climbed aboard the train, along with a dozen or so locals wanting to get to the coast. It was an open iron ore train, and they immediately thought they'd done the wrong thing. It would have only cost a few dollars to keep going by bush taxi, but no, Alex had wanted to do this and it became a test of their relationship.

The daily temperatures reached 50 degrees and at night it was bitterly cold. The winds were so strong that they worried they might be blown off the top. The night skies were as brilliant as back in New Zealand, Fiona thought, but for Alex it was mind-blowing. Never did he think there could be so many stars in the sky. During their first night, they dug shallow pits into the iron ore with their bare hands to get a little protection from the wind. Apart from the brilliant night sky, it was close to unbearable.

Conversations, as always were intense. They had to reserve their talks until the train slowed to a snail's pace or thereabouts, because if the train had any speed at all, it was hard to hear each other above the din. During one slow stretch, Fiona told him that she learned more about the cruel atrocities of the twentieth century than ever before during her time in Africa the previous year. In particular Rhodesia and South Africa were countries where the cruelty of apartheid and the forever present racial hatred, violations to human rights and oppression were all shocks to the system. In her thoughts of late, she felt these existed throughout the entire world though, from South Africa to Australia, and from the United States to Europe. There was no country exempt.

'I learned more however with apartheid as a backdrop, like the hair-trigger margins with which we in the twentieth century live,' she told him. 'I saw how today's technology with our supersonic planes and nuclear warheads, could spell disaster at any moment, and in any country.'

The train had picked up speed and talking became too difficult. Again the dust flew around forcing them to close their eyes and mouth. Years later it would be written up by the Lonely Planet Africa book as being the dirtiest train ride in the world. It was a terrible few days. At the end of their 700 kilometre, three-day journey, they were a combination of tan and black from head to toe. Some of their clothes were so filthy that they had to throw them away.

In Nouadhibou, they were greeted by a gentle Atlantic sea breeze, but the taxi they hailed to get them to a hotel wouldn't stop for them, so they walked. Luckily they were welcomed by the hotel owner, and were able to clean themselves up a bit and to wash their clothes, but it took several attempts to get properly clean, and months later their clothes still bore the dark shades of iron ore as a continual reminder of a trip they should perhaps never have done.

Now in Nouadhibou, they decided to have a day or two off. They'd had their first argument on the train and needed to heal the wounds. It didn't take long, so deeply in love they were falling. They made love here with the windows open and the sea breeze gently blowing across their naked bodies. They went nowhere at all this first day, just rested and made love again and again. Alex had a little bottle of Grand Marnier he'd bought for a special occasion. It had travelled thousands of kilometres in his rucksack. During the afternoon, he found it, and amongst their romantic games, poured some of it carefully into Fiona's clavicle and to her joy, licked it out, then poured some into her belly button and did the same. Then she took the bottle and found places on Alex's body. It was pleasure at its absolute best.

The following day they wandered around town, spotted some seals, saw the graves of many ships and went to the market, where they noted the large number of unrefrigerated stalls selling huge chunks of meat and at others fish with flies buzzing around constantly. Apart from this there wasn't much else to do, so they found out where the bush-taxis left from and the following day walked there for the next stage of their journey.

It was early morning and the taxis were filling quickly. Fiona and Alex had to bargain constantly with each of the taxi drivers they found. Eventually they found one who was legitimately going to their destination and hopped in with about ten others. These old Peugeots seem to be able to fit a lot of people in with extra seats in the rear of the station wagon area and all the luggage on the roof. The bucket seats in the front had been removed in favour of a bench seat and this seat alone fitted four people. It was going to be a crammed but adventurous ride. Their destination was Nouakchott, capital of Mauritania. From here they would change taxi and ride to the Senegalese border. It was a very long day of travel through mine fields where they were warned not to tread. Going for a piss involved women one side of the taxi, men on the other. Walking any further might be your last step.

At the border with no taxis permitted to leave after dark, they camped on the side of the road, ever vigilant of their safety.

Next day after a restless night, they were on their way to Dakar, the capital of Senegal, in another cramped car, this time a beat-up yellow Mercedes. They planned to stop a while in Dakar and get out to the Ile de Goree, an island just a short distance from the capital.

A night resting in Dakar was the best thing to do for them at this stage. They got a hotel room in the middle of town and fell into bed exhausted. The next day they caught a ferry out to the island. Immediately they saw the architectural influence of the various nations who had ruled here: the Portuguese, Dutch, English and French. Sadly the island has a history relating to the slave trade, but what greeted Fiona and Alex was a quiet and peaceful place with no cars, no roads and little stress. Colourful bougainvillea adorned every garden, every house.

Locals greeted them upon arrival offering their rooms for rent. 'This is how they do it on the Greek islands,' said Alex.

'How do you mean?' asked Fiona.

'People greet you at the wharf. There they hold up cardboard signs with hotel names on them.'

'Here they grab you by the arm and speak French really fast,' Fiona laughed.

They ended up getting a small room in a beautiful house close to the water, unpacked and went for a swim at the only beach on the island right next to the port. The air was warm and so was the sea, about the same as each other, they thought.

'This is gorgeous,' Fiona said to Alex.

'I need this after the past few weeks,' admitted Alex.

'Let's stay here a while please, honey.'

'Honey, you called me honey. No-one's ever called me that.'

'Don't you like it?'

'I don't know. It just seems weird. Until you came into my life, I'd never been called anything but Alexander. Now I'm Alex and today I'm honey.'

They both laughed and splashed each other playfully, Alex dunking Fiona at every chance he got.

After their swim they spread out their towels, and lay in the warm Senegalese sunshine. They were both very content. The tough part of their travels seemed to be over for the time being.

The next day Alex got his sketch-pad out and drew his interpretation of the island architecture.

'Would you ever like to add colour to your sketches Alex,' Fiona asked.

'No that'd mean I'd have to carry colour pencils. I like to travel light. I can always add colour at a later date, or use these to do new paintings altogether.'

In the house where they were staying previous travellers had left books. A small book with a blue cover caught Fiona's attention. It was called *Jonathan Livingston Seagull* and as she had just finished her book she swapped it for this one.

'You're the book man, Alex. Have you ever heard of this title?'

'Give me a look. No I haven't. Richard Bach, never heard of the guy who wrote it either.'

'It says it was only published last year.'

'Yeah it looks brand new.'

'I look forward to reading this,' Fiona admitted.

Within a couple of days she had. Whilst reading it she continually read excerpts to Alex making him keen to read the book after she had finished it, which he did.

'I can see why you wanted me to read it Fiona,' Alex said. 'It's a beautiful little book, and surprisingly jam-packed with wisdom. In recent years I've read books by some truly great philosophers and scientists too, but I'd have to rate Jonathan Livingston Seagull in my top ten, maybe not for anything but the sheer pleasure of reading however. But brilliant.'

They stayed on Ile de Goree for just on a week and then caught the ferry back to the capital. On the way into the harbour, Alex noticed all the shipping containers. 'Hey look at that.'

'What?' Fiona asked.

'The shipping containers all lined up over there. People are living in them. Look some of them have balconies.'

'Now there's an idea for the future,' Fiona stated.

'How do you mean?' asked Alex.

'Homes for the poor. I can see that sort of thing being useful in the future, low-cost housing for the young, for students. Join a few together and you could make a decent house.'

The ferry pulled into the wharf and within minutes the two of them were walking up the hill into town to find a place to stay. Having not looked around when they first arrived the previous week, they really wanted to get to know Dakar now. They found a place and booked in, then went roaming around the city. They both looked out for each other as they had been told there were many pickpockets around. Fiona and Alex were savvy travellers though. They knew to keep their eyes open, and their intuition warned them when something was amiss.

Dakar was an interesting place. While on the island they had taken part in a drumming session. Here in the capital they did again. In West Africa drums are very important in the music of the people.

After a few days they again moved on. They began to wonder if they'd keep going all the way to South Africa, but their recent week on the island allowed them to be refreshed completely from the arduous journey which had led them there.

They found themselves travelling again in a bush-taxi the relatively short distance to the southern border of Senegal to The Gambia, where a ferry would take them across to Banjul the capital. The country had not long gained independence from Britain and Dawda Jawara transitioned from Prime Minister to the country's first president.

Fiona and Alex soon headed down the coast to Tanji, a simple fishing village but as it had little accommodation they travelled further. The country only has a 45 kilometre coastline and is actually not much more than a river leading a few hundred kilometres inland. It's Africa's smallest country sandwiched in between north and south Senegal.

Their bus terminated at Gunjur which had a large smoke house, as fish were abundant but again few commercial places to stay, so they ended up with a family in a very simple mudbrick house with no running water or toilet facilities. Outside in the dirt was a well with a semi-enclosed corrugated iron structure for limited privacy and a pit toilet nearby. Alex noted how dangerous the toilet appeared with just a rough piece of corrugated iron placed over the hole. It was daunting to use it, such was the level of diligence required so as not to fall in. The accommodation was good enough though and there were mosquito screens on the windows which they appreciated.

They stayed two nights spending most of the time at or wandering along the nearby beaches. They'd been told about the many varieties of birds in the country and were not disappointed. Everywhere they walked they spotted birds they had never seen before.

This was the smiling coast and there was no doubt about it. Nearly every single person they met had a constant smile on their dial, as Fiona humorously referred to it.

'This is a country I could easily spend some decent time in one day,' Alex admitted.

'I suppose I could too,' replied Fiona, 'There's a lot to like here, not just the smiles, but the genuine friendliness of everyone is a delight to experience.'

'And the kids calling us 'Toubab' all the time.'

'Yeah and have you noticed how they all have road sense?'

'It was the same in Kabul, India, lots of places. The kids just seemed to have a natural ability to respect roadways.'

From The Gambia they travelled to Casamance, southern Senegal, and onward into Guinea Bissau where they hired a boat with a skipper and went sailing in a traditional vessel, designed more for fishing than sailing but with a mast and sail that allowed for a greater area to be fished. It was a great idea Alex had and one which thrilled Fiona no end. After they came ashore, Alex sketched the boat resting on the shoreline.

Again they felt like a break from travelling even if only for a few days, so they decided upon Conakry after talking with other travellers who'd come from there. At the time, Guinea was a Marxist dictatorship under the rule of Ahmed Sekou Toure and as a country it was a place to watch your back. Fiona and Alex were advised not to go out after dark. One night they did though and sure enough they were robbed, and at knifepoint. Luckily they only had to hand over their money which didn't amount to much, and as they'd left their passports in the safe keeping of the hotel manager, they didn't have to worry about those.

The subsequent visit to the police station though was memorable. It was a filthy godforsaken cesspool, as Alex referred to it later, with cells full of criminals and everything carried out in full view of those locked up. There was no privacy for interviews and no privacy for the inmates either. Their toilets were in full view of all those outside the cells, including Fiona and Alex and whoever else was around. They couldn't get out of the place fast enough.

'Thank heavens we only had a bit of cash stolen from us. I wouldn't have liked to stick around explaining a serious theft, like passports and traveller's cheques,' Fiona admitted shocked at what they'd just experienced.

'We were warned not to go out after dark,' Alex reminded her.

'Yeah but it was only just dark and we were only going to the restaurant along the road,' Fiona said a little sad at the whole event.

'I don't think he'd have used the knife. Tourists have money.

You can't blame the locals for trying to get some of it.'

'I suppose so,' Fiona admitted sheepishly. 'A few more boarding houses or hotels wouldn't go astray. I found the people too lethargic last time, not everyone, but a lot of people just sat around on street corners. A few of them should get together and start a business. There's opportunity, limited though it is, but there'll be more travellers coming. They'll never stop.'

Over the months that followed they travelled all the way down the West Coast of Africa through countries like Guinea and Sierra Leone, where they just loved the rainforests. Also to Liberia and Ivory Coast, a successful coffee-producing country, then to Ghana where they visited the newly opened Mole National Park, the largest wildlife reserve in West Africa at the time. The elephants were astonishing, as were the antelopes, hippos, monkeys, buffaloes and everything else they were lucky enough to encounter.

After Ghana they passed through Togo, Africa's second smallest country after The Gambia. Then in Benin they marvelled at the huge baobab trees and discovered that it was the birthplace of voodoo. They heard that there was an annual festival of voodoo in the beachside town of Ouidah. In Nigeria they experienced the aftermath of a three-year civil war and were glad to be free to travel and see the countryside in relative safety. It had the largest population in Africa and, here more than anywhere before, Alex and Fiona noticed the incredible number of citizens who appeared to be just sitting around doing nothing.

After Nigeria, they spent some time in Cameroon working on a mission for orphaned children. They only stayed a week or so, but it had a profound effect on both of them. The health care was poor and the hours everyone worked were never-ending. After a week of almost non-stop labour, Alex had had enough and Fiona was inclined to agree. The place simply needed twice the staff.

In the former Zaire, recently renamed Republic of Congo, they learned of the vast difference between this country and the

DRC, The Democratic Republic of the Congo where civil wars had been under way for years, and where in years to come, it would be referred to as the home of Africa's World War.

In order to travel further south to their destination Johannesburg, they had to get through Angola, where for over a decade a war there had been waging too. In the end, due to continual advice not to travel anywhere within the country and certainly not to try to go through from north to south, they hitched a ride in a plane from Brazzaville to Lusaka. It was time for a rest. Eight weeks of constant travel where the only respite had been the occasional swim or visits to national parks to spot wildlife, landing in Lusaka was to be a welcome break. It was home at the time to the African National Congress, South Africa's major anti-apartheid organisation, and also a safe haven for African nationalists. In the ten years prior to Alex and Fiona's arrival, the population of the city had doubled, so they saw the result of many new buildings and neighbourhoods having been built.

It seemed a pleasant enough city. A new theatre had recently been opened at the university. Named the Chikwakwa Theatre, it promoted plays that sent a clear message for social change. Alex and Fiona attended a play there in their first days in the city. It was a dramatic production in three acts dealing with the then Prime Minister of Rhodesia, Ian Smith, and his fall from grace with soon to be British Prime Minister Harold Wilson. The cast was entirely black making for some rather confusing and at times humorous performances.

Lusaka was a vibrant city with construction projects on every city block. It gave the appearance that the country was moving forward at a fast pace. A few days of exploring museums and markets saw Fiona and Alex heading to the bus station for a ticket to Salisbury the capital of Rhodesia. They stayed at the youth hostel, twenty minutes' walk from the city centre, but each day ventured in to the Monomotapa Hotel for their

55 cent lunch which included a giant burger, salad and chips. Such things were so unimportant really in the whole scheme of things, but joining others from the hostel for a cheap meal and a good laugh seemed an excellent idea. It was an activity they took part in nearly every day they were there.

Their African wanderings came to an end in the middle of winter when they ended up in Johannesburg. If they were going to get to the Greek islands for summer they'd have to make haste. As South Africa was in the grip of apartheid they didn't want to hang around anyway. By now Fiona had spent nearly a year in her two trips through Africa and Alex had spent well over six months. They went to a travel agent recommended to them from someone staying at the Super Soper Shed, a boarding house in Hillbrow and bought their ticket. They chose a date five days away and made a quick trip by air-conditioned bus to Cape Town and back. Then they flew out to Athens.

CHAPTER NiNE

A lex took Fiona to all the highlights of the Greek capital: the Acropolis, Parthenon, Omonia Square, Syntagma Square, introduced her to Ouzo and Retsina, to souvlaki and octopus and after a few days, caught a ferry to the island of Paros. He immediately took her to the village of Naoussa where they rented a small room overlooking the tiny harbour, taking daily excursions on foot to villages like Kolimpithres and Lagkeri.

'I couldn't imagine a more perfect place in all the world,' Fiona said categorically. 'The magnificently friendly people, the absolutely delicious food, the clean whitewashed houses and to top it off being introduced to all of this by you, is just perfect.'

'Thank you, I hoped you'd like it.'

'Like it, I love it, just like I love you.'

'Could you spend some time here Fi, I mean like the whole summer?' Alex asked.

'We'd have to get some work.'

'Do you want to?' Alex enquired further.

'Why the hell not!' Fiona answered emphatically.

And so over the next few days they caught buses in every direction to small and large villages asking about the possibility of work and at the same time seeing the island quite thoroughly. They were offered a number of positions, amongst them washing dishes and cleaning rooms. Alex was even offered an unusual job in Parikea, using a mechanical device to pump water from the harbour onto the streets next to the classy hotels so that the dust wouldn't blow in on the guests. It paid one hundred drachmas an hour, about two US dollars, which was a bit better than the other jobs, but the local hoteliers wouldn't allow a girl to do this job so it was only offered to Alex. After a little consideration they decided against this one. Two Australian guys soon snapped that job up.

Their favourite place was Piso Livadi on the far side of the island but nothing was offered there. In the end they chose a dishwashing job in Naoussa and made a deal with the woman who had rented them their room which allowed them to get a good discount if they paid for it a month in advance. They didn't always work at the same time on the job but they still had plenty of freedom to swim at the various beaches on the island, to ride bicycles which had been loaned to them by their boss, to catch the occasional bus to inland villages like Lefkes and to generally have a magnificent Greek island summer.

They were regularly invited to parties and festivals, joining in with the locals singing and dancing. A weekly highlight was when the bouzouki player arrived at the restaurant. Every Saturday night he would play from seven until midnight and sometimes beyond. As they both worked this shift, they were not only part of the kitchen staff, they were also part of the music. The musician's name was Lambis, the brother of the restaurant's owner Kiriakos, and occasionally Kiriakos would join his brother and break out in song. Usually, within minutes, every customer was singing or dancing or both.

'What a life we're having,' admitted Fiona one Saturday amidst the delightful mayhem of music and moussaka. 'I can't say often enough how this country, this island is so perfect.'

During the summer, Alex met a local artist and struck up a conversation about art. Alex promised to show him his drawings. They met at a small and recently opened art gallery in the main street. The gallery was called Manoli's Art Gallery and Manoli loved Alex's work. So impressed was he that he invited Alex to display some. Within days, they began to sell, so Alex immediately drew more of the popular scenes, churches and fishing boats, and the art started to sell better than Manoli's art. This sparked an idea within Alex which he couldn't wait to run past Fiona.

'What would you say we search for a place to have a shop, our own shop, where we could sell my art and your poetry?'

'What and stay here on Paros?' she asked.

'Maybe. We both love the place.'

'Wait a minute. I was hoping that before the end of summer we might travel to some more of the islands and who knows we might even find an island we like more than Paros.'

'Hard to believe,' Alex added.

'Why don't we just look, not do anything definite this summer, but have it up our sleeve for next year if nothing better comes up?'

'Okay,' Alex said. He was so easy to get along with. Even when he was excited about getting something like his own shop started, Fiona could take a step backwards, make him see the sense in not rushing into something, and he'd immediately see the light.

They worked as many shifts as they could over the rest of summer, and at every opportunity Alex sketched typical Greek scenes: churches, fishing boats, fishermen repairing their nets, octopuses hanging from restaurant railings, in fact anything that attracted his attention. At Manoli's Art Gallery he was offloading his drawings at the rate of several a day during the height of the season. Some were framed, others were not but by the end of August he'd been able to put aside a tidy sum. Together with the wages that he and Fiona were earning, they were able to save over 300,000 drachmas equivalent to over a thousand New Zealand dollars, as Fiona calculated. It had been a very worthwhile summer.

They did look at a few shops in the backstreets of both Parikea and Naoussa in case anything caught their eye, but in the main street, the rents were too high to justify and in the back streets, most of the tourist trade of the 1970's didn't venture. They decided to wait and as Fiona had wanted, to look beyond Paros.

They quit their job before the end of summer, so as to visit other islands before the cooler weather hit. Alex had wanted all summer to get back to Ios and his friend Polychroni and so this was his first suggestion. Fiona was happy to go along with his wishes. The reunion with Polychroni was better than Alex could ever have imagined. He immediately invited them to stay which they were happy to. Polychroni took a liking to Fiona straight away as did Alex with Polychroni's wife Lelia. They were a great group, instant friends.

Polychroni wanted to know all about Alex's travels over the past years and of course the books he had read. Fiona and Lelia would leave the two of them to their discussions, which often went late into the night. Polychroni was continually impressed by Alex's wise manner and worldly knowledge. When Polychroni worked, Alex spent every hour in his library. Fiona was somewhat neglected but had a wonderful two weeks meeting many of Lelia's friends and going on long walks with her.

The time eventually came for Fiona and Alex to depart their company. At Polychroni's suggestion they headed to an unknown island called Gavdos, south of Crete to see what an almost uninhabited island felt like. It was a long journey via Naxos and Santorini, both of which they spent time in, but upon arrival in Gavdos, they immediately knew that it was too quiet and remote even for them. There were less than a hundred permanent inhabitants, but it was enjoyable for a few days.

It was getting towards the end of summer though, and Fiona and Alex decided on a little European adventure prior to winter. Alex phoned his mother, something he only did these days on her birthday and put forward a suggestion that they meet for a family get-together prior to his planned trip to New Zealand to meet Fiona's family. His mother suggested they meet at a Swiss village called Brienz on the shores of the lake of the same name. She had been offered a position as advisor to the Swiss developer who was building a unique open-air village depicting the architectural styles and living methods of the Swiss over the centuries. It was a prestigious position and one she was very proud to have been offered. In the years that Alex had been away her business had received great acclaim across Europe. Her German, Swiss and Dutch cooking methods had been featured more than once in exclusive culinary and travel magazines and she now had a small chain of patisseries throughout the Netherlands.

It was the Swiss government that had put the developer in touch with Alex's mother because of her extensive knowledge not only of Swiss cooking but also of the differences between various cooking styles across Europe. It was with a certain amount of trepidation that Alex finally met up with his family after all these years away, but as it turned out it was the most wonderful reunion imaginable. Not only were his mother and father able to travel but both his sisters and grandparents came too. Every one of his family loved Fiona and the ten days together were stupendous. Days were spent out on the lake in various boats and ferries, walks in the mountains and visiting the site which in years to come would become Ballenberg. Both Fiona and Alex were more than impressed with the designs of the buildings in the proposed village. They could see the fantastic educational potential in depicting the architectural styles, cooking methods and way of life of Switzerland over the centuries.

Before they all parted, Alex's mother admitted that she was going to accept the Ballenberg job, and that the two of them could return and stay anytime.

It was a sad goodbye the day they went their separate ways, Alex's family back to the Netherlands and Fiona and Alex off to New Zealand via destinations they had no idea of. In the end they flew out of Zürich to Bangkok, had a few weeks in Southeast

Asia and then caught a flight to Auckland in New Zealand.

Fiona's family home and apple orchard was on the South Island just outside the adventure capital of Queenstown. They arrived in early November on a perfect spring day. Her parents picked them up from the airport but were a bit subdued. They had to admit to them that the reason they weren't their normal selves was that her grandfather had passed away the week before and the funeral was the following day. It was her mother's father and the last of Fiona's grandparents. Fiona was shocked and overwhelmed with sadness. She'd been very close to him all her life.

'Mum, Dad, I'm so sad.'

'We know darling,' her mother replied. 'Your grandfather was a magnificent man. I don't think he fully recovered after your grandmother died.'

'How did he die?' asked Fiona.

'It was a massive heart attack. The doctor says he probably didn't even know it was happening. He went in his sleep.'

'It's probably the best way to go,' added Alex.

The funeral was a sad affair. People came from far and wide as Fiona's grandfather was both successful and highly admired in the Queenstown community. He'd had a good innings. At eighty-five, no one could complain that it wasn't a long life.

Fiona and Alex spent a fortnight with the family and with picking season just around the corner the two of them were invited back to assist. They knew it'd be a good opportunity to top up their savings, so they said yes. As Fiona's grandfather's car was in the garage and not being used, her mother offered it to Fiona and Alex if they wanted to see the countryside until they were needed for the apple picking. So for six weeks they drove around both the North and the South Island discovering much of the beauty which New Zealand offers. They went back for Christmas and by then the family had returned to their normal jovial selves.

Fiona's brother came over from Sydney with his wife and kids and it was a very happy household. Two weeks later the apple harvest began in earnest. New Zealand wages in the 1970s weren't bad so they were able to save quite a bit. Being the best time of the year for painting Fiona's father offered them the additional work of painting the house, an opportunity they immediately jumped at.

On their days off they enjoyed many of the adventure sports the Queenstown area had to offer like white-water rafting, parasailing, hiking in the mountains and more.

One day Fiona's father called the two of them in to the house for a discussion.

'I need to talk to you about your grandfather's will,' he started. 'You'll be pleased to know that you're included in it. He's left the house to your mother and me, but everything else is to be shared between you and your brother. He has some very healthy investments.'

Fiona looked back and forth between her father and Alex not knowing what to say.

'The solicitor,' her father continued, 'has suggested that you may well be sharing in over a million dollars.

'He never lived like a rich man, Dad,' Fiona said surprised.

'No but he had a very clever mind for the stock market. What would you do if it was half a million dollars that you received?' her father asked.

Again Fiona looked back at Alex. 'Well, we're actually thinking,' she started a little gobsmacked, 'just toying with the idea, of opening a shop of some sort in the Greek islands. We even looked into rentals.'

'Well, you certainly wouldn't have to rent would you?' her father stated happily.

'That's for sure. Imagine how far that money would go in Greece,' Fiona said.

'Don't put all your eggs in one basket,' added Alex. 'There's all sorts of possibilities. You could set yourself up for life.'

'That's right darling, take Alex's advice. You could buy a low maintenance flat in town and rent it out for a steady income for example. Do the Greek thing as well and invest some money just like your grandfather did.'

'That sounds good Dad. This is all very sudden. Did you have any idea what was in his will?'

'Not until the solicitor called,' her father replied.

'I'll look into what his best portfolio was and see if it's still performing well. A small amount in shares wouldn't be such a bad idea.'

While working on the house that afternoon, Fiona and Alex had a lot to talk about.

'This could change everything,' said Fiona. 'But I'd still prefer to have grandad back.'

'Well do you *want* to go back to Greece next European summer? It's only a few months away. You might prefer to stay here.'

'Definitely back to Paros, but first let's start looking at flats here. We don't have to buy straight away but we should start doing our homework.'

Fiona's mother came out from the back door and called, 'Cup of tea for both of you?'

'Sure Mum, thanks.'

They all sat down together and Fiona's mother began, 'It's good news isn't it darling?'

'Yes, but as I said just now to Alex, I'd rather have grandad back.'

'So would I dear, but he had a fulfilling life. He helped everyone he came into contact with, right up to the end.'

'It's a pity I didn't see him just one more time though,' Fiona said sadly. 'I was so looking forward to seeing him.'

'He spoke of you so often, read all your letters ... his and ours. He was so proud of you. And we are too, you gorgeous girl. To travel in Africa as a young woman is pretty gutsy. I'm so glad you've got Alex though now. I'll be much more relaxed if you go off again and have him by your side.'

'Have you spoken with Dad in the past hour?'

'Yes he told me you might go back to Greece. If you do darling we'll come over and visit you. I've always wanted to see Europe. This might be our opportunity.'

'I'd love that, Mum.'

'Yes that'd be great. Europe is so different to this part of the world,' Alex offered.

'Actually there are many similarities, the hills, the green, just not the people and the history, Mum.'

'It's so exciting Fi,' her mother added.

The next weeks were spent searching for investment properties so that when her inheritance came through, she'd be prepared. She had her eye on two different apartments, both two bedrooms and one bathroom, sufficient if ever she needed to live in it herself, and perfect as an investment in the meantime.

When the solicitor phoned with news of the inheritance, the whole family was flabbergasted. None of them had imagined how successful the investments had been. Fiona and her brother shared in 1.6 million dollars.

'It's like winning the lottery,' she told her parents over a celebratory dinner.

'You've got enough to buy both those apartments darling,' her father said encouragingly.

'I might just do that,' she added.

The following day, she put in an offer on both apartments, and both were accepted. The following month she owned them outright and had a steady income stream from semi-permanent tenants. She invested in a couple of different stocks and put the rest in a long term account earning good interest, but had more than enough to return to Greece with to buy a shop and whatever else they thought would be a good idea when they had thoroughly looked into it.

They returned to Greece and went from island to island from early May to late June, searching for an island they might like to call home for a season or two. Santorini came close last time, but still nothing measured up to Paros, not for either of them. So they returned and before long decided to buy a shop on the waterfront that had real street appeal as Fiona put it, in Parikea and an old house across the other side of the harbour in the region of Krios. The house belonged to an old man in the village whose name was Manolis. It was a popular name, sometimes with the 's' at the end, other times not. There was no electricity and water had to be drawn from a well, but it was the clearest water imaginable and the house looked right over the harbour to the port in one direction and to the harbour entrance in the other. It was less than a minute's walk to the beach in front of the house and the total land was 5 hectares. The price for the shop was just under US$5,000 and for the house and land a little over US$20,000. They were ecstatic when everything went through without a hitch.

It was well into August before they owned either of their purchases, not enough time to get a business up and running for the remainder of the summer season, but plenty of time to work on both. Fiona wanted to get a garden going at the house. Alex wanted to get the water and electricity connected, especially if they were going to spend the winter there.

Everything had gone so smoothly with the plumbing and the shop's registration and so on that Alex felt a hurdle approaching. Sure enough, the electricity couldn't be connected until a number of poles had been erected between the last house that had electricity a kilometre away, and theirs. The rigmarole involved in organising this took most of the winter months during which time, they had to put up with a very old and inefficient heater and candles and lamps for light. Still there was plenty of time therefore to snuggle up in bed and do what came naturally.

By mid-January the electricity was connected and their tiny house became more liveable. In spring, they planted some vegetables on the lower side of the house which could be gravity-fed with the rainwater from the roof, stored beside the house in tanks and if and when that ran low, the well could be called upon as a highly reliable back-up. Catching rainwater from the roof was not a common practice in Greece then, and they turned a few heads when they did it, but it was a very good idea.

Alex had spent every spare moment sketching and painting Greek scenery and the subjects he knew would sell well. His drawings in Manoli's gallery had sold out, but both he and Manoli decided to cross-promote each other by having a limited number of each other's works available in their respective galleries. By now both he and Fiona had a fairly good handle on the Greek language.

At Easter, they opened the doors for the first time. Only Greek visitors came to the island at Easter. It was still well before the tourist season, but on their opening weekend, they sold the first item, a large painting of the church at the harbour entrance, the one that Alex first sketched years before, which he'd redone, larger and in colour.

The season that followed was highly successful. Since their time in New Zealand, Fiona had put pen to paper often, writing her free verse poetry as well as short stories inspired from her travels. She'd found a small New Zealand publisher willing to print a thousand copies each of two books of her poems. One was entirely from her experiences in Africa, the other and her favourite was a book with a definite antipodean flavour. Both books sold well as did Alex's paintings. Fiona saw the need for a range of cards on the island, so using dried wildflowers she'd make them while manning the shop. Eventually, in the years that followed, she'd write a short poem in some of them.

Fiona also started attending flute lessons shortly after they opened the gallery. Moreover, her parents visited during the second summer and finally had their European adventure, spending three months on the continent, several weeks of which was on Paros. Fiona and Alex shared everything they loved about the island with all those lucky enough to join them, first Fiona's parents and over the years many others ... and they shared with each other the spectacular sunsets, the glistening moon upon the waters of the Mediterranean, the twinkling lights of distant Parikea which they could see from their home and so much more. Every single thing was a pleasure, even the sounds of the ships' horns when they came into the harbour and moments later the dropping of their anchor, certainly the aromas of sage, chamomile, wheat and barley as they walked home the half-hour journey each night after they closed up—and they *did* walk for the whole year until they bought their first ever motor bike: a little 125cc Suzuki. But even after they bought it, they still walked a lot.

Alex started an art class for aspiring artists the following season and for many years opened the studio the same week they opened the gallery. After the second summer however, they decided to leave for the winters and from that year on, they spent only the summers on Paros, travelling the world during each European winter. Both on the island and when they travelled too, they would meet the most interesting characters, sometimes highly intelligent, occasionally very quirky, but found when they themselves weren't beckoned into in-depth conversations, they'd beckon others. In doing so, a plethora of subjects was encountered. An astonishingly diverse and engaging atmosphere was thus created. People could instantly see that the two of them were intellectuals, and the fact that they loved each other dearly was immediately evident.

Highlights to their lives were many. On Paros almost every day was a highlight. Elsewhere it was usually the concerts they attended and the people they met. One very memorable evening was in November 1980 when they were in Munich and went to a Leonard Cohen concert without tickets. It took three hours outside in the snow asking every person who arrived, *'Haben sie ein extra carte bitte?'* 'Do you have an extra ticket, please?' They finally got the tickets and went in to a most phenomenal evening of song. Years before Alex had met Leonard on the island of Hydra in a coffee shop. Little did he know then how famous this singer-songwriter would become.

Another highlight was when Alex and Fiona visited Alex's mother and father at Ballenberg after they moved there. His sisters had grown up and left home. His grandparents had died and the family businesses, both the shoe shop, the patisseries and factory, had all been sold, setting his parents up for life. They'd bought a lakefront apartment in Brienz where the family had holidayed years before and his mother was in charge of all the cooking in Ballenberg, not a huge job, but a very important one. The four of them had a fantastic time together. Fiona and Alex visited them regularly over the years that followed but his parents never came to see them in Greece.

Polychroni came from time to time to Paros, sometimes alone and other times with his wife Lelia, once even with his sister Maria. It was always a good reunion. Alex also visited him a few times on Tinos.

The 1970s and 80s saw Alex and Fiona grow towards middle age gracefully. They opened their second art gallery on the neighbouring island of Antiparos, the same year that Tom Hanks bought a place there. They built a larger house on their land a little closer to the beach too. They kept the old one for nostalgic reasons however and to house their guests if large numbers came all together.

Over these years Alex had often been asked to show his works at various major galleries in Europe, but had always declined. In 1985 though, at the age of 37, he gave in and showed his works in Berlin to great reviews. What followed was a series of shows in Paris, Copenhagen and London. He continued to refuse to return to his homeland even though he could now, without the threat of punishment by the authorities.

His sisters and their families came over to Paris for the opening of his exhibition. He appreciated the effort enormously and was able to meet his brothers-in-law, nephews and nieces for the first time. Books had started to be produced containing his art and he received several important commissions. His life and that of Fiona too were truly success stories. She played the flute often and carried it to every country they visited. On Paros she gave private lessons, she had become so proficient.

Each year he and Fiona returned to Paros for the summer and both thought they'd do so forever. They'd open the galleries in late May or early June and close sometime in October. It was always pretty flexible. They had many friends all of whom welcomed them each year with open arms but there was a certain amount of sadness when they left.

One summer a young man came into the gallery and the conversation they had got Alex thinking. He told Alex a story about his former life in the Democratic Republic of the Congo, how his family had all been killed and how he was left to fend for himself, how for years it had been a struggle just to stay alive. Apart from a trip to Egypt, Alex hadn't been back to Africa for many years and that day, he felt an urgent need to return. He spoke to Fiona that evening and together decided it was time to do so. It was 1996. In a little over a year Alex would turn 50 and Fiona wasn't far behind.

In October when they closed the doors of both galleries, the Parikea one they managed themselves, and the one on Antiparos looked after by their friends Dimitri and Georgia, they warned them that a change might be on the horizon.

'What do you mean?' Georgia asked in a worried tone.

'We've been coming and going for over twenty years now to Paros. We need a change. We plan to travel down the east coast of Africa, Kenya, Tanzania, Zambia and see what the journey presents us with.'

'I see,' Georgia replied cautiously.

'Do you want to sell up?' Dimitri asked.

'Maybe the galleries,' Alex replied.

'Definitely not the house,' added Fiona.

'But we'll be back for next summer I think.'

'You're not sure,' Dimitri quizzed.

'We'll keep in touch. We won't do anything rash.'

Their friends were obviously concerned.

CHAPTER TEN

They headed back to Athens for a flight to Nairobi, where they landed a few days after departing Paros. They rarely flew in and out of Paros since the airport had been built. They simply loved being on a Greek ferry, even though the ferries of the 90s were nothing like Alex remembered from the 1960s.

Nairobi, or Nairobbery as it was fast becoming known, was nothing special after Paros, but Mombasa was fun, the vendors on the beaches, the different vegetation, different food, black faces.

'Being back in Africa is exciting, isn't it, Fi?' Alex asked.

'I don't know why it's taken us so long,' she replied, 'and what's this calling me Fi again after all this time?'

'Dunno, just feels right.'

'Can I ask you a question?' asked Alex.

'Sure, go ahead.'

'What are your thoughts on the life we've had over the last twenty odd years?'

'That's a big question,' Fiona replied thoughtfully.

'Are you happy with what we've done?'

'Yes of course, why do you ask?'

'Well this young man came into the gallery a while back. He was born in the Democratic Republic of the Congo and saw his whole family killed in front of him. It got me wondering if perhaps our whole life has been a little selfish, you know, we don't actually achieve much for anybody else but ourselves. All that intense reading and studying the great philosophers that

I've done, and what have I achieved? A couple of art galleries to sell my paintings in. It's not much is it?'

'That's not right,' Fiona stated adamantly. 'Your art, and my poetry for that matter, brings joy to a lot of people, and just think of the in-depth conversations we've had with so many people over the years. I'm sure for many of them, those talks were most helpful.'

'I suppose you're right, but I sometimes feel that I've missed my calling, that I should be doing something more important, really helping people somehow.' He was briefly lost in thought.

'I've often thought over the years that what we're doing is exactly what we should be doing, Fiona said. 'I look at the beautiful sunsets that we share with other people, the talks we have, the hopes we offer, the support we give to people down on their luck. All of this adds up to an extremely positive life.'

'Yeah, I know I shouldn't feel so negative, but I do think from time to time that I could definitely be doing more.'

'Well perhaps this trip to Africa will sort your thoughts out one way or another. Maybe this is the break you need,' Fiona assured him.

'But we travel every year after we close up on Paros,' Alex said.

'I think this time it's different, don't you?' Fiona asked, knowing the answer.

'Maybe you're right,' Alex admitted.

'Every other time that we've travelled during the northern winter, we've done so specifically for a break from the gallery. This time we are actually looking for something different.' She paused, then added, 'and considering selling up.'

'You really want to keep the house, don't you, Fi?' he asked with emphasis.

'Absolutely, I think Paros is where I want to die,' Fiona said. 'And actually, I'm not sure if we should sell the gallery. Perhaps we could just put it in the hands of Dimitri and Georgia and let them somehow run both galleries.'

'That's a thought.'

'I think Dimitri was almost suggesting that himself in our final conversation with the two of them.'

'All our options are still open. Come on, let's go for a walk.'

In the days ahead they returned often to this conversation. They never got anywhere though. It was always the same: *should we sell, should we not?*

Fiona's birthday was coming up, and Alex had the idea of taking her sailing in some sort of traditional craft, so when their bus drove in to Dar es Salaam some days later, he suggested that they immediately head out to the island of Zanzibar. They stayed in the main town for two nights and then caught a bus to Matemwe on the north-east side of the island. There they rented a beach cottage and on the morning of her birthday he took her sailing in a dhow. Both of them loved it: the sapphire blue waters, the inquisitive dolphins and there were fish galore.

Their stay on the island became a bit indulgent. They went snorkelling most days, spotted all sorts of fish: Napoleon Wrasse, turtles, Moray eels, trevally, grouper and hundreds of others. Every dive was different, sometimes on coral reefs, sometimes out off the shelf if the tide was low. They read fine books as they lazed in hammocks tied between palm trees, Fiona admitting one day that Zanzibar was the closest to Paros in her level of enjoyment than anywhere else they'd travelled to over the years.

'Do you really think so?' Alex asked. 'What about Patagonia, the beaches of Brazil, Rapa Nui, the coast of Vietnam?'

'You're right again, every one of those was spectacular at the time, but there's something about the Greek people and island life. After more than twenty years, I still can't actually put my finger on it. It's a feeling I get deep within, a wonderful contentment, an almost overwhelming serenity as soon as I walk off the boat, and it's not only Paros. It's just about any island, but this here definitely comes close.'

'Why do you think that might be?' he asked her.

'It's different. The people have darker coloured skin for a start. I don't like the food as much, but put on a face mask and go underwater, and instantly there's so much more aquatic life. In the Mediterranean, we have smaller fish and less of them. Here there's an abundance,' Fiona said thoughtfully. 'So I suppose it's the ocean that makes this place come close.'

The following week they made the decision to hit the road. Their next destination was to be Rwanda but they were so often warned against it that they decided that going there was not wise at all. It had only been two years since the massacre of hundreds of thousands of people. However, in neighbouring countries, Alex and Fiona came across hundreds if not thousands of Tutsi refugees, first in Malawi and then in Mozambique where they arrived after weeks of travel by bus, boat and bush taxi. Hearing their stories was distressing to say the least. In discussions they had with various people, they learned that the trouble that had led to the massacre had been brewing for decades, and it seemed that part of the problem was exacerbated by Belgian missionaries and officials who favoured the Hutu population, although historically that had not always been the case. Years before they had introduced a system called the *nasal index* where people's noses were measured to identify the superior ethnicity. Many instantly began to suffer the consequences. The Twa pigmies made up just one percent of the population of the country and were practically forgotten. The Hutus had built up their wealth through cattle ownership and outnumbered the Tutsis 8 to 1. The Belgians liked the Hutus. Alex and Fiona heard story after depressing story as they travelled around the southeast of the continent and in particular when they spent a few days in the capital of Mozambique, Maputo, where they'd gone at the invitation of an aid worker. There they heard more terrifying stories.

The aid worker's name was Pierre and the invitation was not just to come to the country, but also to visit the mission he worked on. It didn't take long for them to see there was a real need for everyone who visited to chip in with the work-load. And therefore they chipped in and ended up staying for six months. Alex often thought of the young man from the Democratic Republic of the Congo whom he had met not so long ago who'd seen his whole family killed before his eyes. He was hearing worse stories here though.

After their six month stint, they indicated they'd return, after they wound up their business in Greece. It seemed that the new direction Alex had been searching for had arrived.

They returned to Paros via Johannesburg and Athens and stayed for one more season, during which time they sold their galleries but not their home.

'We've come to a decision about the galleries,' Alex started when he met up with Dimitri and Georgia.

'You want to sell?' Georgia guessed.

With a little financial help from Alex, she and Dimitri bought both galleries, the one on Antiparos and the main one on Paros, on the condition that Alex kept supplying a fair chunk of his art. That summer they stayed less than three months, the need for their help in Mozambique so great.

The mission they returned to, which they referred to as Pierre's but which was actually called Capricorn Mission due to its proximity to the Tropic of Capricorn, was more a half-way house, a place where the real refugees in crisis could have a roof over their heads.

They spent several years on and off in the country, returning to Paros for shorter and shorter times.

During their second year in Mozambique, they started to build a clinic. By their third year it was completed. It was a just small building of three rooms, a surgery, a consultation room and a waiting room. Until then all those who fell seriously ill or were having a difficult pregnancy or the like had to travel nearly a hundred kilometres to the nearest surgery which was only operational two days a week. They built it specifically with the intention that it would help the young, but of course it was open to everybody. They just made sure that the nurses were suitably qualified for paediatric work and in particular children affected by war, so a sympathetic counsellor was employed too. While it was being built, they visited other camps and missions throughout the country.

In all the missions they visited over those early years in Mozambique, Alex and Fiona took little pleasure afterwards in explaining any of the real details they'd discovered relating to life for a child of war, both before having been rescued and afterwards as well, as was the case in some of the camps and missions. What they loved however was sharing their knowledge and making clearer to people who had little idea what trauma was associated with children in war situations. It was somewhat of an eye opener for all sorts of important people they started to meet following the construction of the clinic. The head man of the mission that Pierre worked at, one of six under his control, began to encourage Alex and Fiona to hold talks to visiting dignitaries. Telling people face-to-face about atrocities, Alex became adept at in-depth, eye-to-eye discussions and in turn he started to get known for his directness. For example, he never held back when it came to explanations of rape and torture. He told it as it was.

It was because of this no-nonsense approach from both of them, but especially from Alex, that the two of them were offered the opportunity of setting up a large clinic, a hospital really, just across the Zambian border with the Democratic Republic of the Congo.

'Why not, it's not as if we can't afford the time off,' Fiona said when they discussed it immediately after getting the offer.

And so this ended up being another couple of years of their life, working their skin to the bone not only organising the project, but getting stuck into the physical side too, mixing concrete, digging trenches and all.

They had to do all of the negotiating with the local chief of the district where the hospital was being built, get all the materials, arrange all the tradesmen, and make sure the job got done. This included them getting their hands dirty and skin bare. At the end of the two-year project the hospital was completed. Even all the donated machines were installed, checked and switched on. The gardens were complete including concrete pathways and a partial bitumen driveway.

Opening day was three days before the end of 2002. A new hospital in a remote part of Zambia tends to attract dignitaries from far and wide. Some of these people were known to Alex and Fiona from previous dealings in various places where they had travelled in Zambia and also down south in Mozambique. Some were hard-arsed politicians, crooked in the extreme, others doctors and lawyers, all sorts of folk.

The hospital immediately started taking in children from across the border. Their stories were heartbreaking. They were documented thoroughly by Fiona. Everything was from day one.

Arrival Date: Jan 12, 2003

Age: 14

Sex: Male

I was told to train. I would have to allow myself to be beaten, bashed, stung by bees. I would do anything I was ordered. Then I was trained to dismantle and re-build a gun, over and over for a week. They put someone in front of me and ordered me to kill. I killed.

Arrival Date: Jan 14, 2003

Age: 12

Sex: Female

At first, we killed animals. Then we had to kill our

people ... everyone in our village who was not abducted to start training as a child soldier.

Arrival Date: Jan 15, 2003
Age: 16
Sex: Male
My name is Edward. I am now 16 years. I was abducted at 9 years and spent one year training and fighting. One of my jobs was to carry heavy loads of stolen food which was from the rich countries. It never made it to the people it was meant to help. Soldiers stole this food. One boy complained that he was tired, so the rebels told him to put down his load and the other children were told to gather around him. I had to join in. The soldiers chopped off his feet with a hoe. One rebel, one foot each, and then his hands. The soldiers told us to cut off his eyelids with a razor while they held him. Then his arms were tied behind his back. He was still conscious. Then they hung him upside down from a tree and we were told to box his head with our fists until he was dead. We all cried while we did it. The soldiers laughed and smoked cigarettes. It took many minutes before the boy died.

Arrival Date: Jan 19, 2003
Age: 11
Sex: Male
We were told that our final training involved cutting pieces from people's bodies while they were alive. A village that had been unhelpful in the past was singled out for punishment. Every person in that village was rounded up and brought to our camp. There were three different types of punishment handed out that day and each villager had the task of drawing a card from a hat to determine which punishment he or she would receive. Those too young to

choose had their card picked by a parent. The cards were all hearts from a normal playing deck. Drawing out the king of hearts meant you lost an ear, the queen of hearts a finger from each hand and the ace of hearts meant that you lost your tongue. Some of my fellow soldiers couldn't do this. The oldest was only 15. It was too much to ask. Some boys threw up, others fainted while waiting in line. Those who refused were encouraged just once. If they still refused they were castrated and left to die a slow death when we abandoned the camp later that day. I heard some weeks later that of the one hundred and fourteen villagers who were tortured that afternoon, over forty eventually died. All six of my comrades who refused to carry out the punishment and were castrated, also died.

Alex and Fiona thanked God continually that they didn't have to be the ones who heard these stories first-hand. Some required translating and this was performed predominantly by the doctors. Fiona and Alex wrote them up though and filed them on the computer ... that was depressing enough. The hospital had good success, but medium and long-term accommodation was needed, so they decided to build a camp, a rehabilitation camp for former child soldiers, a place where kids could not only receive physical and psychological treatment, but also a place where they could play games and learn how to be kids again. The first year they had twenty and then thirty tents to house the children and their families who were coming across the border. The second year they had two substantial dormitories completed and they were well on the way to completing the food hall. The following winter, everything was finished. They could now accommodate well over a hundred people, kids on their own, families, anyone who showed up. The tents remained but were from then on used only as a back-up, which became more and more a regular event. With the hospital right next door there was a new ward doubling the total number of beds to thirty.

It was an astonishing achievement for all concerned. Four years before, when Alex and Fiona first came here, it was a dust bowl. There was nothing here at all. It was desolate. They never believed anything could be established, let alone grow here. Thanks to a good well having been dug, and the rains that came during that first year, the whole place survived quite well. With the goats, chickens and a sizeable farm producing most of what was needed, it was a great example of what could be achieved in such an inhospitable region.

In time, the charity group for whom they worked decided it was necessary not just to have a visiting doctor from time to time, but to employ a full-time one. The man who arrived to take up the position was Dr Edward Brown from London. He'd been working with Médecins Sans Frontières for some years and therefore had extensive experience in Africa. Alex and Fiona immediately became friends with Edward and enjoyed the many months that followed until their departure in 2005.

They were pretty burnt-out and were looking forward to a rest in Paros. When they got there, Fiona checked her emails and there was one from her brother in Sydney. For years, he'd been the CEO of a major charity and asked his sister if she and Alex would consider a trip down under to be part of a team organising a bus-load of disabled people in a trip around Australia planting trees.

'Hey Alex, take a look at this,' she beckoned.

'What's up?' he asked.

'Oh there's nothing wrong, but Rohan wants us to come to Australia and help a disabled group on a tree-planting tour.'

'What?' he asked incredulously.

'Seriously, he's developing a plan to encourage people with disabilities to travel around the whole country it seems.'

'Find out more. I've never been to Australia. It might be time,' he said. 'After all our time in Africa, I could do with a real break.'

'What a strange life we have,' Fiona admitted, shaking her head almost in disbelief.

'It'll certainly get stranger if we go to Australia and do this,' Alex added.

In the days that followed, Fiona and her brother wrote back and forth almost continuously. He hadn't actually thought they'd want to come and help, but was keen to encourage them after they showed initial interest. A few weeks on Paros catching up with their friends and tidying up the dusty house and they were off again. This time they used the airport and flew to Athens where they purchased a stand-by flight.

They arrived in Sydney and were picked up by Fiona's brother Rohan and taken immediately to his Kirribilli home overlooking the harbour towards the bridge and the Opera House. His wife Amy was away.

'Do you realise, my dear brother, that in the past month we have travelled from the wastelands of Western Zambia to the Greek islands and now here to Sydney?' Fiona asked.

'Yes I do realise this. But you two are used to it by now, I'd say. Thank you so much for agreeing to come. If it's okay with you, tomorrow we'll get straight into the planning,' Rohan said.

'You don't muck around, do you?' Alex stated.

'Well, if you guys didn't want to be part of this plan, I had to pick two of our staff, and with the seasons to consider, we don't have much time to get this started if we're going to do it this year.'

His plan was this: a group of disabled people would leave from Sydney heading north in a bus towing a trailer full of saplings. They would meet up with various groups across the length and breadth of the country all doing the same thing. These people would join them for short periods as they toured the country, planting trees in their local areas and helping them to stock up their supply as they reached them. Their common purpose was to replace the trees chopped down by two hundred odd years of destruction.

There'd be nurses on board in the main group to assist with the various problems that might arise with the disabled passengers, and they'd compare notes on the successes as they progressively met the other groups on their way around the country.

They met with a fair share of opposition to the plan. People said things like: 'Who the hell do ya think y'are?' and 'You'll never do it.'

At the entrance to every town along the journey, they would plant one of the saplings and erect a small sign saying: 'This tree commemorates a journey, a journey of disabled people into the future. This tree is one of a million trees planted in the summer of 2005–06 by disabled people across Australia.'

By the time they departed, there were three buses, not one, each with twenty-five disabled people aboard; five nurses and a doctor came too. There were a number of major sponsors and therefore 100 percent of the costs were to be covered.

Additionally, the drivers and co-drivers were experienced tour guides able to pass on to everyone the knowledge they'd attained from years of conducting tours in the remote parts of the country. And they too were all first-aiders.

Hooked up to each bus was a trailer with roughly a thousand saplings. They carried all sorts of varieties, but mainly eucalypts. An automatic miniature sprinkler system was fitted to each trailer so as to supply the trees with water along the way, especially in the hotter regions.

They didn't just plant one tree in each town. They planted dozens in some, and at nearly every roadside rest area throughout the country they planted more. A documentary was to be made, so at a lot of the towns up the east coast, news teams were gathering footage as well as the documentary team in one of the back-up vehicles. It was an incredibly slow process. At the beginning of the journey, every single one on board wanted to be involved. This caused minor logistics problems. Getting seventy-five disabled people, a few of whom were in wheelchairs, off a bus in weather of all descriptions, was somewhat of a chore for the nurses and staff, but by the time a few days had passed, they had it down to a fine art, and the initial problems were a thing of the past. People took it in turns to get off and perform the planting tasks.

The highlight of the first couple of weeks was Fraser Island, the largest sand island in the world. The whole island is a botanical garden, rich in a large diversity of species. From the huge satinay trees, the woodland giants, to the tiny insect-eating plants that cling to the shores of the lakes, the group was treated to such variation.

They learned that the Aborigines in former times discovered that this environment offered beautiful, succulent foods, from the shellfish prolific in the blue ocean waters to the flowers of the Xanthorrea, which when soaked in water provided them with a refreshingly sweet drink.

These people from long ago lived in harmony with their environment. Their keen observations showed them that when the fern leaf wattle began to bloom, the island's kangaroos were expected to be fat, and when the wild passionfruit was ripening, the carpet snake could be eaten.

Some of the plants on the island, such as the macrozamia, an ancient plant from the primitive cycads, were poisonous. The Aborigines would soak the bright red fruits in running water for several days allowing them to lose their poison, and then mash them into a beautifully edible delicacy.

They hadn't taken the buses across to the island. Instead, they were picked up by large four-wheel-drive trucks. It was quite an exercise, a joint effort by the national parks service and the army.

They took with them a token number of Brisbane Black Wattle, which only a few years earlier was on the endangered species list.

The four-wheel-drive trucks drove along the white sandy beach which stretched the length of the island, occasionally stopping to enable the national park guides to point out the island's features. They saw the foam bark tree (Jagera pseudorhus), the branches of which were used by the Aborigines of the past to hit the water releasing a chemical from the leaves of the branches, stunning the fish and making them easy to catch. The king parrot and the green catbird also love the fruits.

They were shown the Angiopteris fern, a remnant of the steamy life on earth hundreds of millions of years ago, and learned about the carnivorous sundew plant, a member of the Drosera family, which survives in the swamplands by catching insects. They were shown the melaleucas and paperbarks, some estimated to be 2,000 years old. And they discovered that members of the animal kingdom on the island were equally as spectacular, like the giant earthworm which has an acid-resistant film on its skin, and the acid frogs that have developed a tolerance enabling them to live and breed in the acidic environment of the waters. Their time on Fraser Island was exceptional, one of only three islands they were to get to in the trip.

In some towns, especially in Queensland and the Northern Territory, many of the people who came out to help the planting process were from the local Aboriginal population. They lived in sometimes harsh environments, with limited water and few of the luxuries that city folk had become accustomed to. Their homes were tin shanties situated in dusty outposts. They drove beat up old Holdens and Fords, which, in the city, would long ago have succumbed to the wreckers' hands.

These people of the outback had to contend with long distances, inadequate nursing and bush hospitals with limited supplies, and although most of them suffered only from minor eye diseases and so on, there were others who had horribly deformed limbs and got around on crutches made from eucalyptus branches and other makeshift bits and pieces. And there were other major health problems too.

In the way these people lived, Fiona and Alex saw the remarkable similarities to what they had experienced with the poor of Zambia and Mozambique in their recent travels. Some places it really hit a nerve. When they drove into Fitzroy Crossing, many weeks into the trip, they were welcomed by every person in town and hundreds from neighbouring communities as well. Brown-skinned people covered in dust, with white teeth and bright eyes shining through their tough exteriors. Every one of them wore a smile.

For some of the disabled aboard the bus, this scene was too much. Seeing kids who should have been in wheelchairs, struggling with bits of branches to prop them up, Alex noticed tears forming in the eyes of many of the group. Most of them didn't get off the bus immediately. Experiencing all this was hard. But the smiles on the faces of these outback people were magic, and they won the hearts of everyone.

Fiona and Alex always spoke to each other of highlights. Fiona had kept an extensive diary all her life. Even as a child she wrote her childhood thoughts in the first of what was to become many subsequent journals. But there were lowlights to this journey too. They were on their way west toward Broome, the old pearling town, leaving the bright smiles in the dust behind. They drove all day and arrived at sunset. Seeing the sun setting into the Indian Ocean was an experience few of the group would ever forget. The sun seemed to hover around the horizon for ages, before dipping into an azure sea. One young man had found the going tough in recent days and on the advice of the doctor, had to be flown home. But it was the only time in the entire trip that such an event occurred. It was definitely a lowlight to the trip.

In her diary Fiona noted all the stops including Anastasia's Pool at Gantheaume Point, an almost perfectly round pool that was hand-built by a former lighthouse keeper for his wife, Anastasia.

She was crippled with arthritis and found relief in the pool. One of the bus drivers knew this fact and thought it highly appropriate to bring the group here so as to experience the place.

While in the vicinity, they also admired the magnificent red cliffs and turquoise waters of the region, then all got off the bus to view the footprints of a dinosaur from 130 million years ago.

They discovered as they progressed through their day that one site they couldn't visit was the old Broome Zoo ... now just a ruin of a bygone era. It hadn't been a normal zoo. Instead it catered only for endangered species. Animals and birds from all over the world were housed there, a dream of an eccentric Englishman, Lord McAlpine.

Fortunately though the bird observatory was still in existence, so the group went there. Migratory birds from Siberia used this as a stepping stone and the area had become regarded as the most significant site in the whole country for shorebirds. Over 800,000 visit annually.

It was a full day, but it wasn't over yet. It was the night of the full moon and they were able to experience a natural phenomenon which was caused by the moon rising over the exposed mudflats of Roebuck Bay at extremely low tides, creating a beautiful optical illusion of a staircase reaching to the moon. It was a fitting end to an exceptionally interesting day.

Then they had to endure one of the longest legs of the journey. Western Australia is like that: lots of distance between towns. But the group had been advised what to plant in these remote parts of Australia, shrubs like the Bassia paradoxa, a brilliantly white flowering plant. In Port Hedland, over a hundred people joined in, a dozen or so from the disabled community including blind people. Some very elderly people joined in too. In towns like this, the part the group played was minimal. They'd get the whole thing under way, and then it was the responsibility of the locals to keep up the momentum and plant the remainder of their allocation of trees. In Port Hedland, 5,000 trees had been allocated. In the two days they were there, they planted the first five hundred, and then they left. It was terribly hot and quite depressing. At least in a few years, there'd be a bit more shade in some parts of the city.

They visited other towns on their journey south: Exmouth and then Carnarvon where the whole group sat under the trees by the Gascoyne River and had a picnic lunch. Carnarvon was one of the towns where their stocks were to be replenished. They had a day of doing almost nothing. It was a well-earned rest.

By the end of the week, they were nearing Shark Bay and the world-famous Monkey Mia, home of the dolphin, the dugong and the most extensive sea grass meadows in the world. It was Christmas Eve. They were going to spend Christmas with the dolphins.

They turned off the highway at Overlander, a place comprising a service station and a store, and headed west to one of the remotest parts of Australia's coastline. On the way in, they passed something which was both unique and significant.

Stromatolites, a life form from 3500 million years ago, grow and prosper in the shallow waters of Shark Bay. The three buses pulled in and stopped there for a short time. They all ventured down to the new walkway overlooking the shelly beach where they were told by one of the drivers that the word *stromatolite* was a derivation of the Greek word meaning 'bed of stones', and that's what it looked like too. He also told them that the stromatolites were the oldest life form on earth.

'Scientists from all over the world come to Macarthur Basin to study them,' he told the group. 'The cyanobacteria, the microscopic organisms which formed the stromatolites 3500 million years ago, were the first photosynthesisers to obtain hydrogen by splitting the water molecule, thus liberating oxygen into the atmosphere.

'They were able to use solar energy,' he continued, 'to

synthesise simple sugars from hydrogen and carbon dioxide because they had chlorophyll, the light-harvesting green pigment which characterises members of the plant kingdom.

'Their activities created an atmosphere with sufficient oxygen to sustain the air-breathing life forms which are now characteristic of our earth. These simple cyanobacteria prepared our planet for life as we know it and determined the form that it would take.'

Alex found out later that the driver used to bring scientific study groups to the area. The knowledge obviously rubbed off.

Later that afternoon they arrived in Monkey Mia. There to greet them were the dolphins.

This group of intrepid tree planters was positioned around the beach and jetty and became mesmerised by these marine mammals which seemed to be talking to them. When they arrived, they were just swimming quietly around the foreshore. After the group had been positioned at various spots along the beach and on the jetty, the dolphins began to jump and dance and whistle and sing. At that moment, both Fiona and Alex could see that the dolphins most likely knew this group of people had an important mission.

The camping area had been transformed in recent years, and there was little remaining of the original camp built many years earlier by Wilf and Hazel Mason. Nowadays it was four-star camping all the way. For Fiona and Alex and many of the others, it was the best night of the entire trip.

They sat for a long time under the stars that night talking about the journey, about the trees that had been planted and about their disabled friends who they were travelling with, how strong and capable they all were, how they had risen above their disabilities.

'None of these people could possibly have dreamed a few months ago, that they'd be out here doing this,' Fiona said at one stage. 'What freedom they're experiencing!'

'Yes, seeing young adults with cerebral palsy and various other disabilities being pushed and helped through the campground to see the dolphins was beautiful to watch.'

Looking at them with their Akubra hats in a harsh environment such as Monkey Mia, was an absolute thrill for Fiona and Alex. What they were experiencing was almost beyond description. The contact between humans and dolphins displayed real harmony. There was so much happiness.

'You know Fi, today, watching the interaction of our group with the dolphins, the way the people talked and giggled and the manner in which the dolphins seemed to respond, I was reminded of a quote by Mahatma Ghandi.'

'What was the quote?'

'He said: *Happiness is when what you think, what you say, and what you do are in harmony.*'

'It was pretty harmonious today, wasn't it?'

'Absolutely,' he responded contentedly.

As Fiona and Alex sat looking out across the waters to Cape Peron, they noticed in the water at their feet tiny, glistening phosphorescent plankton. They began to make little whistling noises and clicking sounds with their teeth. Fiona pulled from her pocket a faulty cigarette lighter she'd picked up from the beach earlier and flicked the flint. The plankton seemed to answer by moving erratically to their noises and flashes by flashing their phosphorescence back at them. When they stopped, so did the plankton. They amused themselves for ages doing this. It was lots of fun.

After hours of watching the heavens and the sea, talking about lots of subjects, the midnight hour approached.

'What we're doing here on this journey of ours is vitally important. If we don't do things like planting trees, and having interaction with other species, it won't be long before there are no opportunities at all to be had. If the world dies, her inhabitants will die along with her. There'll be nothing left for anyone. The whole world will be a barren wasteland if we don't start to think.'

Just then, a dolphin came gently to the surface a few metres from where they sat, and made the softest, subtlest little sound.

'Do you think dolphins talk from their minds as well as their voice-boxes?' Alex asked.

'It's highly likely, whales do,' she replied. 'This one here probably knows what we're talking about.'

'And yet we kill them, call it scientific research like some mad countries do. Now there's another thing I'd like to do before too long.'

'What's that?' she asked.

'Fight for the rights of animals.'

'You're doing more than enough in recent years to help the planet,' she stated firmly.

'We both are,' he added.

It was late when they headed back to the campground. Everyone was deep asleep. They too decided to hit the sack. It had been a wonderful start to Christmas, like no other before.

That night as Alex's head hit the pillow, he had a strange feeling as he drifted off. Suddenly there was blood everywhere and he could feel the surging of the ocean. There was a tremendous noise of engines and machinery. It was deafening. Above it however were mournful cries. He turned his head and saw three minke whales, one merely a young calf, being towed backwards behind what appeared to be a 'slaughter vessel'. They'd been harpooned, all three of them. The explosive-tipped harpoons had killed the baby, but the older two were struggling and crying desperately. Their insides had been literally blown apart. As Alex stood above the slipway of the Nisshin Maru factory ship of the Japanese whaling fleet he could do nothing but weep.

He described the dream to Fiona next morning, asking, 'Why do we still do this?'

There was no answer.

Their tree planting, shrubs this time, along the foreshore of Monkey Mia began shortly after breakfast. All day Alex thought about the dream of the night before. He felt really sad most of the day. Every time he saw one of the dolphins playing in the shallows, he thought of their cousins the whales.

They planted solitaire palms as well as the shrubs in the dolphin garden at Monkey Mia rather than the eucalypts, but towards the end of the morning, they decided to plant some of the eucalypts too behind the park so as not to detract from the view. They now had a tree expert with them, and at all the various pick-up points, the trees for the following days and weeks which arrived had been even more carefully chosen prior to shipping.

After lunch, the group rested for the remainder of the day and watched the tourists playing with the dolphins. Everyone took the opportunity of meeting a dolphin personally, some of them with wheelchairs parked in the water, others walking in and patting them. What a Christmas. They exchanged gifts in the late afternoon, but none was as special as the experience of being with these friendly creatures.

The day after they farewelled the dolphins and were on their way. Everyone had been deeply moved by their meeting with these exceptional creatures.

Before they left, the lady in charge of the dolphin information centre presented every single one of them with a poem written thirty years earlier by the then curator of the park, Wilf Mason.

He was there in the early days when dolphin visits were not so common. The poem read:

> *In a world of seeming darkness,*
> *filled with famine, bombs and fright.*
> *At a place called Monkey Mia*
> *there's a tiny speck of light,*
> *where a special kind of feeling*
> *coming from the sea.*
> *Can light our darkness*

and help the world be free.
Where the dolphins in the water
show a friendliness to all.
It makes no difference rich or poor,
young or old or small.
They keep coming in to see us
with their ever friendly grin,
showing us the joy of life
and the freedom we can win.
This speck of light we speak of
we should never let it die.
We should fight to keep it glowing.
Everyone must try.
We must nurture it and cherish it
and always keep it warm.
For this little speck of light we see
will one day be the dawn.
So we ask you all to help us
keep this dawn aglow,
nurture it forever
until we make it grow.
As the dawn of love and freedom
climbs ever ever higher.
We bless the love and friendliness
of the dolphins of Monkey Mia.

Monkey Mia was by far the highlight in the entire state of Western Australia. They only planted two hundred trees and shrubs there, but what the group learned in the presence of the dolphins was very important. Everyone raved about the stay there for the rest of the trip.

From Australia's most westerly point, they headed inland a bit and then south via Kalbarri, Geraldton and the windsurfing centre of Lancelin where they watched the sailboarders jumping waves. Then they hit Perth. What a surprise that was.

By the time they arrived there, the news of their journey had become really big. Thousands of people lined the city streets as they drove through the downtown area and made their way to the hotel where they were due to stay.

There was cheering and clapping, whistling and singing, even dancing in the streets. News cameras and reporters were everywhere.

Perth was a wonderful city with hot days tempered by afternoon sea breezes to cool the temperature down. There were no restrictions to swimming like up north where the sea-wasps and crocodiles made going into the ocean hazardous for everyone.

Here instead, swimming and sailing, skin diving, kite-surfing and sail-boarding were all a part of life, twelve months of the year, not that many of the group could do these things but it was great to watch those who could.

They planted a thousand trees in Perth and a further two hundred on nearby Rottnest Island. Several hundred Perth locals, many of them disabled, helped with the effort. It was all very well-planned with the landscaping already finished and only awaiting the arrival of the team and the trees they were to plant.

They stayed in Perth for three days and celebrated the New Year there. Fireworks over the Swan River, it was now 2006.

Before they left, they visited the International Gravity Wave Observatory at the University of Western Australia. It was at the forefront of worldwide gravitational research. Physicists here were able to investigate the formation of galaxies, to observe black holes and to understand space and time more thoroughly than Einstein himself could have imagined. Scientists now had the opportunity to uncover the origins of existence itself. Visiting the observatory was a mind-boggling experience for all of them.

After their three days in Perth, they headed east to the gold mining areas of Kalgoorlie and Coolgardie. From Coolgardie they headed back toward the coast so that they could visit the world-famous south-west region where century-old jarrah, karri and marri trees grew wild in national parks.

They planted trees in most towns along the way. Towns like Pinjarra, Dwellingup, Manjimup, Katanning, Bunbury, where they again saw lots of dolphins, and even a pretty little place called Denmark welcomed them with open arms. Wherever they went they encountered caring people who had developed a true love for trees and all things green.

In this south-west area of Western Australia, they learned about the endangered species of bird known as the Western Bristlebird (Dasyornis longirostris), and they planted many of the endangered Rose Gum (Eucalyptus rhodantha) and the Gungurru (Eucalyptus caesia) to encourage their return.

From Denmark, they followed the coast to Albany where they met up with the West Australian disabled community's bus. Fifteen people varying in age from four to seventy-seven had just completed the inland road from Mount Magnet via Dalwallinu, Northam, Corrigin and Katanning winding up in Albany to coincide with their arrival.

They partied all afternoon and into the evening. It was a lovely night there in Albany, the moonlight dancing on the waters of King George Sound. The following day, after planting several hundred trees in various areas around town, they bid the West Aussie group farewell and prepared for the longest leg of the trip, via Esperance and Norseman across the Nullarbor Plains to South Australia. This leg was to take over a week.

Esperance and the nearby national parks were barren but beautiful. Cape Arid—the name said it all. The colour of the waters in this southern region was amazing. It was a turquoise green. The sandy beaches were white and windswept. They planted trees everywhere they went.

Further north, in Norseman, they again picked up trees brought in by train and truck from Perth, and then headed east across the Nullarbor. The trees chosen were from the hakea family, known for their hardiness. They had to be tough to survive in areas where rain was sometimes not seen for years on end.

Nullarbor, in Latin, means 'no trees', but in tiny pockets across the desert they partially changed that.

The Nullarbor was an arduous part of the journey. A few of the cerebral palsied people fell victim to various illnesses, mainly fatigue, and at Eucla, the group made an unscheduled three-day stop so that they could be treated at the new bush hospital there. They'd have loved to visit the Koonalda Cave, but it was too dangerous so they just looked at a DVD about a recent group of speleologists and the work they were engaged in there and in other locations throughout Australia. It was a boring place to be stuck in. All their sick friends recuperated relatively quickly. All that most of them needed was a rest.

It was during this extended stop at Eucla that the team met a great character. He was an old bushman, dusty and tanned from the desert sun. He only had one leg but this didn't stop him doing all the things he wanted to do. He could even ride a bicycle, and it looked so funny when he did it carrying his crutches under his arm. With one leg he could ride as well as anyone. Alex was glad when he came up to the group in the pub dining room on the first night, as he really wanted to meet the guy after seeing him riding along the highway earlier in the afternoon on his rusty old bicycle with handlebars high and a grin from ear to ear. It was a fantastic evening of laughter. This bloke could really tell a story. He was an inspiration, showing them all what could be done even after losing a leg.

Such was the situation everywhere Alex and Fiona went over the years. They met captivating characters all over the world. 'I've got to write a book about them,' Alex often said. He of course kept a diary as always, but it was not as extensive as Fiona's always were. From Norseman to the West Australian border, there'd been no towns. They'd only stopped at rest areas. Dry, barren but by no means lifeless. The bus drivers were incredibly knowledgeable when it came to showing the group what the desert offered. In an area that many people call lifeless, they were shown just how full of life it was. Plant and animal communities lived in total harmony, each species with their own important role to play.

Once across the border, they made their way via Ceduna and Streaky Bay to the famous Eyre Peninsular, where years before, sheep in their millions had been farmed.

With the decline in world demand for wool in the early 1990s, many farmers went to the wall. At the beginning of the decade, 20 million sheep and lambs, more than the total human population of the country at that time, were slaughtered, to date the largest slaughter of sheep in Australia's history. Having little or no market for the meat or for the wool, farmers were forced to shoot their sheep in great numbers, and bury them in mass graves. Alex found this extremely depressing, as did Fiona.

'Farmers need help much more often than they get it,' he stated firmly.

When they passed through the area, they experienced the expanding alpacas goat industry. Related to the llama, this creature, although smaller, was renowned for its strong though delicately soft fibre. In just three years since the decline of the wool industry, the alpacas had just about replaced the sheep in some areas. In other parts of Australia, they were to see how the modern farmer was farming kangaroos. Low in fat and high in protein, it too had changed the face of the Aussie farm scene, but not before a lot of controversy. People simply couldn't understand how Australia could farm their national symbol.

And there was talk of further changes. The ostrich, a flightless bird originally from Africa, was also being experimented with. Cholesterol-free meat and a good strong hide, coupled with fine feathers, made this creature a possibility for future consideration on the Australian farm.

South Australia was a real eye opener for them all. Each of the Australians on board had grown up with the idea that Australia rode on the sheep's back. No longer was this so. The group was experiencing a fundamental change in the Australian pastoral industry.

At the time, Alex wondered how many changes were to take place in other parts of the world as well. In the United States for example, the wheat belt had for years been under threat. So many countries relied upon US grain yet the yield had dropped every year through the 1990s and now into the twenty-first century.

Not long after they left the Eyre Peninsula, they made their way via Port Augusta and Port Pirie to Adelaide, where again they were met by a number of disabled people all willing and eager to join in and help with the tree planting program which by now had become big news throughout the entire country. Twenty thousand people lined the streets of this garden capital of the south. It was one of the most exciting days imaginable. Many of the disabled group cried with happiness. It had at last dawned on them just how important other people considered what they were doing. They were greeted by Jonathon Porritt when they arrived at their hotel. Jonathon had originally organised the Tree of Life project in the garden city and, several years earlier, had set up a Forum for the Future. He'd also been a past director of Friends of the Earth. In Adelaide he met great success, just as he had everywhere else he travelled. These days he lectured in all sorts of world venues and almost never put his pen to rest. He was an inspiration to everyone on the trip.

They stayed in Adelaide a week, getting their strength back after the long journey across the desert from the west. They planted every second day and visited Kangaroo Island by catching the vehicular ferry at the end of the week. Spotting koalas in the trees and kangaroos in every field was enormous fun for all of them.

They planted trees in a superbly organised fashion in Adelaide. There to assist them were landscape designers and advisers, professional gardeners, horticulturists and thousands of willing hands. Adelaide was a garden city before they arrived. When they left, it was even greener.

From Adelaide they headed into Victoria, visiting the grape-growing areas of Renmark and Mildura. On the way, they learned of the over-usage of water by the cotton growers of the Murray-Darling and how the river system was slowly dying. There was massive change on the horizon however.

They visited a town called Roxton where the sewage was used to feed 60 hectares of River Redgum saplings in the late 1980s. By the time they passed through the town some twenty odd years later, the trees stood 20 metres high, a monument to a brilliant idea. Every time a toilet was flushed, a tree grew a little more.

Shortly after, they experienced how the local farmers were replanting the mallee areas, endeavouring to cope with years of destruction and deforestation.

A new outlook had developed in the final decade of the twentieth century. Areas once rich in topsoil had suffered greatly in the name of progress, much of the topsoil having disappeared in the years since white settlement. Now, a few years into the twenty-first century, the problems were partially being rectified through planting and regeneration.

They helped. Like everywhere else they'd been, they planted trees by the hundreds and thousands. In the mallee, they again planted eucalypts. Perhaps some of the numbats, bilbies, barred bandicoots and quolls, animals that once flourished in the Murray Mallee, would one day return.

By the time they reached Melbourne, they'd once again run out of supplies, but their stocks were to be replenished, not before a gigantic reception however. Braving the rain, a hundred thousand people showed up to greet them. It was truly an amazing spectacle.

By now, the journey had made international news. There was NBC, CNN, ITV, BBC and several more news services hovering around.

They stayed in Melbourne for a week as they had done in Adelaide. The Tasmanian group had been planting their allocation of trees for the month leading up to this, and came across Bass Strait to coincide with their arrival. They'd concentrated on the Morrisby's Gum (Eucalyptus morrisbyi), another of the endangered trees.

The Melbourne disabled group had been up in the alpine areas planting White Sallee, the Snow Gum (Eucalyptus pauciflora) amongst others and they too joined the group after they'd been in their city for a short time.

They planted trees most days, but as some of the team were becoming a bit worn out by the arduous journey, many rested every other day, leaving the planting to the not-so-tired Tasmanians and Melbournians.

From then on they stayed with the main group, all through East Gippsland and into the southern areas of New South Wales, where the now five bus-loads planted an abundance of Yarra Gums (Eucalyptus yarraensis) and the Small Leaved Gum (Eucalyptus parvifolia). Then they hit Canberra.

It was here that they met up with the Canberra disabled community group who'd travelled throughout the entire western areas of New South Wales. They'd covered such isolated communities as White Cliffs, Broken Hill, Bourke, Brewarrina, Nyngan, Dubbo, Cootamundra, Wagga, and hundreds of other places. In Canberra, the national capital, they rested again before heading back to the coast and on up to Sydney.

It took them more than a week to get there however, this being the most populated area of the country, the south east that is. There were towns every few kilometres, places like Merimbula, Bermagui, Narooma, Tuross Head, Moruya, Bateman's Bay, Ulladulla, Currarong, Gerringong, Wollongong, Kiama and finally Sydney, but there were literally dozens of other towns and small communities as well, each with their own particular pre-planned tree requirements, and all with friendly people to greet and help them. You see, by this time, communities had plans printed out for the group's arrival. This made everything a lot easier. No decisions had to be made. They just followed the plan. It had happened in a lot of towns in Western Australia too, but here it was every single community.

They stayed in some of the prettiest coastal locations in the world. Alex's favourite was Bermagui, Fiona's was Narooma.

Then in Sydney they arrived on a glorious sunny day to a tickertape welcome. Sydney hadn't seen anything like it since the Olympics.

The Prime Minister was even there to greet them. Rohan was on the podium as the main speaker. The Greens MP Alicia Webster was MC. There were a lot of speeches. The most memorable was primatologist Jane Goodall whose speech received the biggest applause. Dr Goodall was invited in her capacity as a UN Messenger of Peace. She spoke of many important subjects relating to the future of the human species. She pointed out that we are not being ethical in our decisions. She congratulated all those who had been on this journey to help improve our world. 'You have improved the lungs of our planet with your expedition,' she said. Her most poignant words however were regarding the animal kingdom: 'If we cry, we cry the same tears as the animals...we are all one family. We must continually strive to save our world'. Alex and Fiona made no speech, but they did accept a plaque as a token of appreciation from the charity group.' Farewelling the members of the group with whom they'd travelled all these months was difficult. They'd all experienced something that would remain with them forever. It had been a special time for every one of them, and the nurses, doctor, drivers and of course Alex and Fiona were ecstatic with the outcome.

CHAPTER ELEVEN

Fiona had promised her mother in their regular contact during the trip around Australia that she and Alex would visit soon after the trip was over. First though, unsurprisingly they wanted a day or two off.

They spent an afternoon on glorious Sydney Harbour, and the next day, spent the entire day in the Ku-ring-gai National Park catching a ferry from Palm Beach. The national park on the other side of Pittwater was so beautiful and peaceful, so close to the city, yet a picture of wilderness.

Before they left Sydney they visited the organic gardens for the disabled, which were situated all around the metropolitan area. There was one at the Spastic Centre at Allambie, another at the Horticultural College at Ryde, and one at the Quadriplegic Association Headquarters, where regular fêtes were held to sell their produce.

Then it was off to New Zealand. Both Fiona's parents were now in a retirement home and her father was quite frail. It was a warm reunion and many of the other relatives came down to Queenstown so as to join in on the celebration of their return. Fiona and Alex privately discussed the chance of either or both of her parents dying before their next trip back, so they stayed for many weeks, taking them out most days on little trips.

As they'd said that they'd return to Zambia and continue their work, they eventually said good-bye and did what was the norm for these two, that is, start travelling again. They knew it was their life, but others sometimes found it hard to understand how they never stayed in one place very long any more. Her father reminded Fiona once or twice while she visited and voiced his disapproval. 'You've got a home here darling, several in fact, and we'd love to have you around.'

She wanted to use Alex's words when he said this, but didn't. 'There's not enough years in a human being's life to see the whole world, so there's no use standing still.' Alex often said this to people who questioned their continual travels. She bit her tongue instead and gave her father a loving embrace.

From Auckland they flew to Sydney, then Perth and across the Indian Ocean to Johannesburg, the most efficient way of getting to Zambia. First though they went via Mozambique to check the progress of the clinic and were happy that nothing was amiss in the years they'd been away. They'd set up a trust fund administered by a trustworthy lawyer to cover expenses not met by the charity. It was refreshing to hear how many success stories there had been.

Two days later they were in Western Zambia at the aptly named Lumwana Mission Hospital. Unlike the hospital that President Lungu commissioned, this one actually had doctors and nurses and drugs in the cabinet.

It wasn't actually in Lumwana though. It was closer to the border so that refugees didn't have to travel so far on foot once they escaped the Democratic Republic of the Congo. It was an absolute joy for the two of them to return.

They'd lost track of how long they'd been away. Life seemed to be getting a bit like that. They did so much travelling that even they became confused as to which month was which and what year it was. They were welcomed by staff and patients, residents and the few locals who'd arrived, including a family from Solwezi, a town to the east. The father was a mechanic, or fancied himself as one, and actually brought his family out there with plans of starting a business. His plan worked as there were the vehicles that visited and the vehicles in the hospital and camp, as well as the pumps all of which he serviced. But what a place to live. In his home town he couldn't get a job, and they became destitute. This was their last chance. Alex and Fiona took a liking to him as soon as they met him. And the family were very loving towards each other, another thing Alex and Fiona liked.

The kids, with no other school to attend but the one in the camp, did so. By being a part of such a school, they were definitely learning different lessons, interacting as they were with refugees.

With the arrival of this first local family, it appeared to Alex and Fiona that they were experiencing the birth of a new village. In time, the number of families grew; some from within the camp were forced to become permanent residents because, sadly, they had nowhere else to go.

Over the handful of years that followed, thousands came through the camp and the village numbers swelled to a hundred. A new village had certainly begun.

Alex and Fiona continued their moving around the globe, Paros during some summers, but sometimes they wouldn't even get there. In Zambia they spent a few months here, a few months there. In time, all but one of their parents died, the final one remaining being Fiona's Mum whom they still got around to seeing from time to time on the south island of New Zealand.

Alex and Fiona had both applied for temporary residency in Australia at the end of the big tree-planting expedition and both were successful. They could pretty much come and go as they liked nowadays.

CHAPTER TWELVE

On his next return to Australia from Zambia, Alex was invited to address a refugee group in Sydney. He had to replace the keynote speaker due to a tragedy that had occurred. He discussed the subject possibilities with Fiona and what they came up with was the story of Mbaye who was meant to speak to the audience, but due to tragic circumstances, no longer could. The convenor of the conference introduced Alex who slowly and deliberately walked up the steps to the stage. The location was the Sydney Town Hall.

'Ladies and Gentlemen,' he began, 'thank you for the opportunity of sharing the following story with you all. Refugees as we know come from all corners of the globe. Their arrival brings mixed feelings and varying levels of success. Sometimes there are failures, failures not only of the refugees themselves, although that's rare, but of the country that was supposed to welcome them, to look after them. My story is the story of Mbaye, who was a refugee from the Democratic Republic of the Congo. He was born in a small village two days walk from Mongbwalu in the north. For many generations his family were simple farmers, but in his grandfather's lifetime and his father's too, they made a small living from mining gold because it had been discovered by Belgian fossickers. Mbaye's father and grandfather worked hard for many years digging for the precious metal. They toiled for long hours each day. Due to illegal taxes and levies however, their wage was small and life for them was very difficult.

'The family never had an abundance of anything except love. Yes that's right, love. It's the one biggest thing that makes Africa tick. They were as close as Mbaye dreamed his own family would one day be, if and when he was lucky enough to find a wife and to start a family. His mother would always care for each of the children, holding them close, protecting them from the wind and dust storms so prevalent in that part of Africa where they lived their humble existence. They never had enough food or clothes and the children were always hungry, but the young ones thought that was normal. Everyone in their village often went without food. Sometimes, during periods of hardship, they would eat nothing but cassava roots with the occasional treat of some boiled rice, which as poor and near destitute people they devoured with pleasure.

'When Mbaye was just 7 years of age he was taken from his village and never saw his family again. The day on which he was taken was Friday, the traditional day of prayer, and it was from their tiny prayer shelter, a small covered area with no walls, that he was abducted. At the time of his abduction he was the youngest of six children. In the years that followed he often wondered if his parents had more children, but he never met anyone from his village so he never found out.

'The men who took him away trained him in many things. First he learned how to use guns. He learned how to take them apart and clean them, how to put the guns back together, how to load them and of course how to shoot. He also learned how to kill. In the early days of his captivity he was very frightened. The first few months after he was taken from his family he cried every day. He hardly slept. After those early months it became normal for him to perform terrible things on the men, women and children of his country. All the other boys who were training with him committed atrocious things too, so in time they all felt that what they were doing was right.

'The older boys had to shoot people and burn their houses. Sometimes the houses belonged to people they knew, even their own families and still they were ordered to kill them. It was not uncommon for them to be ordered to eat parts of the dead bodies too. The young soldiers didn't know why this was necessary, but the punishment for those who refused was death, often a very slow and painful death which the other children witnessed almost on a daily basis. These killings were often carried out for everyone to watch. The fortunate ones were shot in the head and died instantly. Others were not so lucky. Some were burned alive. The worst Mbaye saw was when a senior soldier, who was very drunk, tied a boy behind a jeep and dragged him bumping around the compound until he died. He could still hear the boy's cries more than twenty years later, every time he thought about it. Other children though told even worse stories than this.

'The camps were always very busy with soldiers coming and going, trucks, jeeps and more children being brought in to begin their training. Every camp was the same, usually with large wire fences around the whole area to keep them from escaping. Often there were young girls too. Mostly they were used for sex. In one of the worst camps Mbaye saw a girl have her eyes gouged out for refusing to have sex with a large group of the soldiers. After they gouged her eyes out, they committed depraved acts upon the child and she died after a day or two.

'The young soldiers would go out from some of the camps and never come back. After a period of burning villages and killing they would end up somewhere different and the nightmare would continue. As a boy of 7, then 8 and 9, Mbaye had no idea how far he had travelled from his family. He didn't even know if he had crossed a border or borders in these months and years as a young soldier.

'He remained a soldier for three years. It was an awful time; every single hour of these three years was a torment, even after the terror became normal. Together with his fellow child soldiers he carried out terrible atrocities upon his fellow countrymen. Then, out of the blue, together with fourteen of his fellow child soldiers, he was rescued. It was sudden and unexpected. They were woken from their sleep by a small team of men dressed in dark clothes, hooded and carrying semi-automatic guns. At first Mbaye didn't know what to think. Who were these people he thought to himself. It became clear quite quickly and each of his friends ran to vehicles waiting at the compound fence, escaping quietly through a hole that had been cut. Driving very fast in three cars they drove away into the darkness. They drove for many hours until the sun came up and then they drove further. They had to stop at a checkpoint with many soldiers and Mbaye became very scared, but these were friendly soldiers and soon after they pulled up at the front of a house with trees and running water to a tap in the garden where they all had a shower. Then they ate and rested for several days. Their life of killing had ceased.

'They'd joined a larger group in a compound with no fences. They'd been brought to Western Zambia. At this camp there were classrooms and fields where they could play football, a game many of them had not previously known. Mbaye was nearing 11 years of age and became quite good at the sport. Many of the boys used their skills of being nimble on their feet to good advantage. He enjoyed every moment at this place, not just the football. His lessons were relaxed and he learned many different things. He learned to read and write and became quite good at expressing himself. He happily learned to do other things children were meant to do, including how to smile again.

'A futile attempt was made to locate Mbaye's parents and the rest of his family. The charity group who had organised Mbaye's rescue also tried to locate as many families of the other children they rescued, but with little success. Some children were re-united with their families but sadly very few.

'Years later they learned that the most likely fate was that those who could not be found were dead. Mbaye suffered a lot while growing up not knowing the circumstances of their deaths, if they had endured pain—which of course was highly likely. When his fellow child soldiers and himself had carried out killings, some of the things the older ones did were too gruesome to think of now, all these years later. His only hope was that if the members of his family *were* killed, they each died quickly. However he still lived in the hope that one day someone from his family would show up, even to far-off Australia, half a world away. He had such thoughts often after arriving in Australia, rescued once again and arriving as a refugee. Studying in the grand buildings and relaxing in the manicured gardens of the university which had offered him a new education, he sincerely hoped this would happen, that perhaps one of his siblings would arrive, but he suspected such a wondrous thing would not occur. He realised every day that he'd had good fortune, that he was one of the lucky ones and hoped that others would enjoy this same satisfaction, the generosity of Aussies. He had the utmost admiration for open-hearted Australians who had offered him this new life, had invited him to a country where there was education and food for all, medical and dental care which was second to none, support groups for every conceivable malady, but it pained him that other countries were not so fortunate.

'Mbaye made friends easily. He was tall and good looking, agile and intense. He engaged his fellow students in healthy debates, discussed at length subjects close to his heart. He intrigued them with stories from his homeland but kept the gruesome details of some parts of his former life to himself.

'Not long after he began his studies, he started to write about his life, not fully realising what he would do with these words when he finished. He knew though that he wanted people in the West to realise that life can be so very different from what they knew. *"Most of the world is not like Australia,"* he wrote. *"In this country there is help for all those in need. In other countries, it is not the same."*

'Being enrolled in a course studying human rights, he began to understand even more that he was one of the lucky ones. *"From my early lessons after my initial rescue where I learned to read, to write, to understand maths and geometry, all through my teenage years and now university, I have learned so much knowledge which I would not have been able to learn, had I not been rescued all those years ago."*

'What saddened him most as he studied was to learn of the absolute disparity between countries of what he considered were truly important things, the total imbalance, as he referred to it. *"It is fortunate,"* he wrote, *"that of all the world's conflicts, none has really reached Australia. My own childhood was taken from me by a regime which was responsible for many, many deaths, 2.7 million of those deaths being children. Millions more of its citizens were killed outright or simply disappeared."*

'And when Mbaye learned of events throughout history as bad as and worse than what his fellow child soldiers and he were forced to carry out, he was shocked.

'He had no idea of course of the mass murders, the genocide carried out by fanatical leaders like Pol Pot, or even Adolf Hitler, because he'd had no real education until the age of 11 and even then such things were not taught. University was opening up an entirely new world to him, and he knew that he wanted to do something vital to help. He wanted to be successful in his chosen career, whatever that ended up being, but not success for the sake of it. He wanted to do a job that counted, to be involved in a profession that did enormous good for his fellow man.

'His studies from that first year covered many atrocities both in modern times and throughout history. He learned things about Africa he'd never dreamed of, like the bizarre ways of leaders like Idi Amin, the butcher of Africa, who was responsible for the deaths of up to half a million people and was so depraved that he kept the heads of some of his victims in his refrigerator and had a team of kitchen staff prepare favoured sections of his victims' bodies for him to feast upon with other favourite foods like roasted goat and Kentucky Fried Chicken.

'And others such as Thomas Lubango Dyilo, the first person ever convicted by the International Criminal Court of Justice in The Hague, now serving a reduced prison sentence and due for release before this decade concludes. He was convicted of ethnic massacres, murder, and the conscription of children as soldiers.

'One of the worst dictators of the twenty-first century was Charles McArthur Ghankay Taylor, the former president of Liberia, currently serving a fifty-year prison term after having been found guilty, at the International Criminal Court, of terrorism, crimes against humanity and the conscription of children amongst an array of other charges.

'And of course Joseph Kony, leader of the Lord's Resistance Army which originally formed in Uganda and, after losing the support of his people, continues to lead a terrifying regime of killing and rape in the Democratic Republic of the Congo, the Central African Republic and southern Sudan. It was *his* army that had abducted and trained Mbaye and hundreds of thousands of other children in the Democratic Republic of the Congo, and who was responsible for the deaths of millions. Often his men would appear at church and prayer services, attacking the elderly with machetes and then abducting those who would be useful to them, including of course the children as soldiers and sex slaves.

'Mbaye's studies taught him about leaders far and wide, leaders of all sorts of countries, military leaders, dictators like Saddam Hussein, Josef Stalin, Leopold II of Belgium, Mao Zedong, some as ruthless as and worse than Adolf Hitler and

Joseph Kony. It troubled him deeply to learn how the human species could stoop to such depths of depravity.

'Opportunities, he learned, had been wiped out by these madmen. His former country was and still is teeming in copper, gold and diamonds, mineral wealth which other countries would give anything for. The soil is rich and grows an astonishing number of high-quality fruits like guava, mango, banana and orange. So rich is this soil that it is said it could feed all of Africa. But it doesn't. Crime and corruption have denied the country of any positive future in the short term. Much of the African continent is like that. Shocking things happen all the time. It perplexed Mbaye to discover why not more is reported about atrocities in Africa in the press. He felt it may well be due to it being put in the 'too hard' basket. Parts of Africa, including the Democratic Republic of the Congo, were just too remote and the horror simply too common.

'And it caused him great anguish to learn that other countries were also responsible for atrocities, places like Burma, Indonesia, Laos, Kurdistan, Nepal, the Philippines, Sri Lanka, Angola, Yemen, Chechnya, Bolivia and Columbia and then the obvious hotspots of madness such as his own former country, the Democratic Republic of the Congo, and Somalia, Sudan, Uganda, Afghanistan and Iraq. He learned that there were many more. Even the so-called civilised countries were in fact not so civilised at all.

'Mbaye discovered that it was not a new thing, the forced recruitment of children to fight adult wars, but he knew it was something that must stop. And with the rise of ISIS in the twenty-first century, he wondered what shocking increased barbarity would infiltrate life in the West. His concern however was for Africa, but he realised the problems went well beyond the shores of that continent. ISIS fighters too are getting younger, he learned. The recruitment of children is widespread, in Africa, the Middle East and beyond.

'As he wrote in his diary and on his laptop he wondered what he could do about all this. So many subjects troubled him. In Africa, it was the corruption and the forced recruitment of youngsters as child soldiers. Here at home, his new home, Australia, he began to see other problems existed. He was deeply concerned about the mandatory detention of asylum seekers which had become the norm in an otherwise fair country. A year or so after his arrival in Australia and just before he began his university course, he'd joined a refugee group and became an active participant in organising events for those lucky enough to be accepted into mainstream Australia. He found it absurd now, years later, that an average of 445 days of detention was somehow acceptable by a nation of free-thinking and friendly men and women. It was one of the many things in a long list which worried him terribly.

'In his first year of studies he'd scored top marks in an assignment. This was the first of many assignments where he scored well. On this first occasion he was asked by his professor to read aloud this top scoring work because the professor saw that Mbaye had come up with such a simple design to fix a big problem. Reading his assignment to the class, it impressed his fellow students enormously. The assignment featured a toilet design he'd thought up after visiting the bush toilets of national parks shortly after his arrival in Australia. As a youngster, he'd experienced the horror of a family of close friends discovering that one of their children had fallen down a long-drop toilet and drowned. *"Children get toilet-trained very early in Africa, almost as soon as they're able to walk,"* he read to the class from his assignment. *"Our toilets are the 'squat' variety, a hole in the ground with some rough timber or stone foot-steps in the better ones, plain old earth in most. The problem is that the holes into which one does one's business vary enormously in size and are often covered with just a simple piece of corrugated iron. Often nobody sees a child heading to the toilet. The child pushes the cover aside and sometimes, in his or her excitement, doesn't negotiate the hole properly, with the result that they fall in. When it is discovered that the child is missing, chaos reigns. An entire family will search frantically until the horrible discovery of where the child went, is made. You see, the toilet hole is too small for an adult to climb through and extract the child, so the fire brigade is called and a grappling hook is used to retrieve the body. It is a terrible way to die, but for the parents it's almost unimaginable the feelings they must experience."*

Children die all too often in this manner in the developing world. Reading about this to his classmates and showing them the design he'd created to alleviate the problem, he received great respect. Quite simply it was an inverted witch's hat which could be retro fitted to any long-drop toilet anywhere. A small person could still fall in but only partially, because the hole at the bottom was considerably smaller than the one at the top. Mbaye hoped one day either to return to Africa and start production of the device or to pass it on to someone else who would.

'Throughout the following years of his course, he astounded his lecturers with his concise method of discussing all manner of subjects and his succinct way of expressing himself with the written word. He kept his private aspirations however to himself. He dreamed of a better world and as time went on felt sure that he was going to do something positive with his life after university. He wanted to help the world with more than just a small innovative toilet design, and this desire was the main reason he'd started to write. *"If I can get others to read my work and to find out a bit about the lunacy of our world, perhaps together we can all help. This, in time, might have an enormous effect. We might even create something beyond our dreams."*

'While *he* regularly impressed his classmates, *they* impressed Mbaye. In one assignment titled *Societal Expectation and Hopes* again he scored near the top of the class; however he personally thought that others in the class deserved higher marks than he'd achieved. The top-scoring assignment was about the changing face of Australia and ridiculed the way in which Australia was no longer the forgiving and welcoming land of former generations, a land of freedom and friendship. His fellow classmate wrote about the new Australia with its non-acceptance of minorities and a government without heart where mandatory detention for asylum seekers had become the norm.

'This method of locking up asylum seekers had confused Mbaye in the past as he loved his new country, a place where he felt very much at home. When he arrived, he experienced none of this compulsory locking up. He was glad to hear that more and more people were doing something about the issue.

'However his concern was still fundamentally with Africa. He wanted to bring African awareness to the masses because he felt that many people across the globe were unaware of what problems existed there, how some of her problems were almost insurmountable and needed a united effort by many to bring about change. Even after all the education, the famous musicians who raised awareness with memorable concerts, the informative books, films and documentaries which had been produced, still on the whole, there was ignorance and ambivalence.

'His hope was that by writing about Africa he could make people realise how dire the situation was becoming. *"It is my hope that this story will change ignorance, at least to a small degree. I'm not putting words on paper,"* he wrote, *"to attempt to divulge the entire story. It would be beyond my skills to do so. However I do want to make a point about the way in which African leaders, whether they are despots, rebels or so-called legitimate rulers, take children of all ages, and yes sometimes very young, like 6 and 7 years of age, and make them fight and do a lot worse than using an AK47 to shoot and kill."*

'With his studies he was beginning to realise though that even amongst his classmates, other problems were a priority to them. He'd have to make a concerted effort to raise awareness of the problems of Africa. He understood that things were not right in Australia, but really the situation was considerably worse in other parts of the world. So, on he wrote, often seated beneath his favourite tree in the university garden shaded from the sun, tapping away on his laptop.

"'Across the world there is an estimated 300,000 children fighting in 30 wars and conflicts," he wrote, "and almost half a million more are in training. More than a quarter of this number are girls, often used as sex slaves. Children are used because they are easily manipulated, tenacious, daring and unfortunately often trusting. Even those who begin to experience doubt as to why they are doing what they do are then often fed drugs which quickly turn their doubt into a reliance upon yet another thing they have no understanding of."

"As well, their captors, superiors—call them what you like—threaten them with harm upon their families or themselves if they refuse orders, and when you learn that on a daily basis they see proof of this punishment occurring, it's easy to understand their compliance, so they succumb and do as they're ordered, fearing the worst because they see the most horrible things in their short lives.

"Right in front of their eyes," he writes, "they witness the people they love being slowly and deliberately tortured, women raped with rifles, men having their penises cut off, their throats cut and their tongues pulled out through

the hole that's created and then let hang down towards the victim's emaciated chest, in front of the children, remember, who watch as the person chokes to a slow death or drowns in their own blood, all for no reason at all, or simply because a village refuses to feed the soldiers as they pass through. Not for harbouring someone, not for fighting or killing or hurting anybody, sometimes just because they have no food, so they politely refuse and suffer the consequences. Other times a villager can simply look at a soldier the wrong way. That's often enough to bring down the wrath of an entire bedraggled platoon on a village of innocent farmers struggling to make an existence amongst the mayhem of a war they don't even understand. Then they're killed, just like that, their village torched, the women raped, and everyone in the vicinity annihilated.

"And who are the guilty ones?" he asks. *"The leaders of well-trained and committed armies, sometimes rampaging rebels, sometimes even leaders who have the respect of their countrymen and women, rulers who have been democratically elected. But also the blame, to a degree, is upon every one of us who does nothing."*

'So what was Mbaye advocating? He considered that perhaps the best method of improving the lives of those affected by war and terror, including the vulnerable young, was simply to spread the word. *"People should openly discuss these dreadful issues, write to politicians, newspapers, talk amongst ourselves, openly, freely, lovingly,"* he wrote. Eventually positive things would begin to happen. It wasn't going to happen overnight, but it *would* happen. *"And regarding those who seek refuge, welcome them with open arms."* There had to be an attitudinal change, a massive one. He felt that people in the West had to begin to learn more about other places, about what happens to people in far-off lands. Life was far from acceptable to so many people all over the world. Mbaye felt that we had to begin to care a lot more for the well-being of the vulnerable. It was Mbaye's opinion that there are enough good people in the world to make a united effort to bring about change, and he knew that there was a lot of change needed.

'He wasn't asking for anything in particular as he wrote daily on his tiny laptop. He was merely making some suggestions, hoping one day they may be published. *"If you want to give money to your favourite charity, do so, though this is not the answer. If you want to hold gatherings for refugees to help them integrate into our society, do so; however this alone is also not the answer. If you want to write to your politicians and remind them of the plight of people in troubled lands, by all means do so.*

"And if a child of yours wants to give a year of his or her life and go to Africa so as to lend a helping hand, then encourage it. Don't say, no, stay at home and go to university. Going to Africa is a university of a different kind where all manner of new lessons will be learned, empathy being one of the major ones. And more importantly in this instance help will be given, perhaps the most valuable help of all, encouragement in the right places. The key is in education, within Africa and outside Africa too. Within Africa we must encourage diversification, innovation. Beyond her shores, we must open the minds of those who have previously looked upon Africa as a basket case, open the minds of people who think Africa is not worth the effort. Africa needs all the assistance she can get, money to legitimate charities, helping hands wherever possible and the spreading of the word of just how difficult life is for many over there."

'Mbaye had the sincere hope that before too many more

years passed, he could witness great leaps forward for Africa, a continent where children whose lives had been torn apart by armed conflict, would be forever safe, where they were no longer forcefully taken from the loving embrace of their families and given guns which killed and maimed. He hoped to see an Africa where people no longer died unnecessarily from preventable diseases, an Africa where people no longer toiled from dawn to dusk for little more than a meal for their families, an Africa where dictators no longer got rich at the expense of their country folk, and an Africa where there was legitimate opportunity for all her people. As well though, he hoped that those who made it to Australia, from all the world's troubled regions, not just Africa, would be welcomed more than they were at present.

'He knew well and truly that he was a lucky new Australian, a young man who'd come from a world of extreme cruelty and brutality to a country of freedom which he now called home. He felt that together all people can make an enormous difference. Just opening our minds and learning about the real problems of our world can bring about change; if at the same time we open our arms too and welcome people who have endured hardship, we'll be creating an exemplary world. Australia could then be the example to other countries which Mbaye thought it should. *"It could be the best country in the world,"* he wrote.

'Each time he sat in the gardens of the university writing his ideas for a better world at his favourite bench beneath the large Moreton Bay Fig, he would close his notes and meditate for a short time, soaking up the splendid and tranquil ambience of the historic place of learning. Then he would walk home to his small flat just a five minute stroll, a few blocks' distance to where he lived.

'Ladies and gentlemen, it is my sad duty to inform you that Mbaye will not be speaking tonight. I am not here to introduce him. A few evenings ago on his short walk home, a group of youths approached him soon after he left the grounds of the university and began to torment him calling him names and making fun of him. We should remember that his life had been full of torment, of having to use his cunning, on many occasions of having to dodge bullets. "Black bastard," one called. "Go home, you don't belong here," another hissed. Moments after the taunting began however, the jeering stopped as one of the youths came up from behind and with a single punch to the side of Mbaye's head, knocked him to the ground, his skull cracking hard against the pavement. This was his final moment. Mbaye had taken his final breath. This was the final injustice from what we are so rightly calling a coward punch. Many of you are refugees. Many of you have gone through hardships which you thought may never end. Many of you have witnessed gruesome murders, mass murders, as did Mbaye. He was a shining light, ladies and gentlemen, a special person who could well have become a leader in his field, and most likely even more, but for the action of a coward, an inconsiderate stupid human being.

'I am privileged to have been able to read excerpts from his diary to you tonight. My work in recent years has been in Mozambique and in Zambia, and it was in Zambia that I met Mbaye. He was one of our earliest arrivals in a camp established to assist children who were victims of war to rehabilitate, to join society again, to be kids again. Mbaye was one of our success stories. He was most definitely a shining light. We'll never know how far he could have gone.

'I do not want applause, but I would like together with you all, to applaud Mbaye.'

The auditorium erupted. Many of the audience were in tears. Some had not until now known of Mbaye's fate. The applause went on for many long moments.

Alex quietly left the stage.

CHAPTER THiRTEEN

Having the opportunity to read Mbaye's diary and notes got Alex thinking. He was now 68. He was the author of several best-selling books, had established an artists' school in Greece and galleries on two of her islands, and together with Fiona had built a small hospital in Mozambique and a rehabilitation camp in Zambia. They had travelled around Australia with a group of disabled folk planting trees. It was an impressive list. Most people would be more than content if they were able to achieve so much in a lifetime, but Alex wanted to do something more.

With the Syrian and other crises in the world of the twenty-first century, he wanted to somehow bring his dream to reality, his dream of bringing people together in order to help themselves rather than relying on others.

So with help from Fiona, he began a letter. In the letter, which he planned to send to various newspapers, he described a two-part plan to help refugees. Before the idea was born, every man and his dog wondered how Australia's 12,000 refugee intake would work. Europe, with the influx of over a million refugees, was really struggling. What to do with a mere 12,000 was a cinch when the nation started to think about it. Now other countries were looking at Australia's example and really taking note. And it was Alex's letter which was the catalyst.

He and Fiona toiled for many long hours over several days getting the wording just right. Then they sent the letter off. After it was published, a ground swell began that just kept growing. Alex really needed to do something big since arriving in Australia and this was perhaps going to be something monumental. He'd already achieved great successes with the tree planting journey and his previous efforts in Africa, not to mention his art and writing.

Basically he had two ideas to help the arriving refugees. The first had to do with the farming community. 'Farmers,' he wrote in his letter, 'are doing it tough, so tough that some, frustrated by their situation, are taking their own lives. It's not just continual droughts that are having a detrimental effect on their livelihoods. Floods too have caused immense hardship in some regions. Then there's the wild dog problem, stock diseases, falling stock and produce prices and in the dairy industry, due to ongoing supermarket milk wars, farmers are having to deal with absurd wholesale milk prices—the list goes on and on.'

The idea he came up with and what he decided to put into the letter to the newspapers was this: some of the refugees could do a year on an Aussie farm, helping the struggling farmers in some way. He said it'd be a bit like doing an apprenticeship and at the same time show the Australian people that they were sincere in wanting to integrate into this great country. They could help with the planting and harvesting of crops, assist with animals, do some fencing, just about anything that farming life could throw at them. This was the easy part. He was sure his idea would take hold in one or two communities, and once a few people saw the benefits, farmers from other communities would want to be a part of the plan. It'd be a win-win situation for all.

His next idea was considerably more complex. This second part of his plan went in the letter too.

During their trip around Australia the group, on a day off, visited the Herberton Museum on the Atherton Tableland in far north Queensland. He'd been really impressed by the place. It was an entire village of buildings and businesses from yesteryear. And of course there was the impressive Ballenberg in Switzerland where his mother had worked for years. In that village, there were extensive examples of Swiss buildings over the centuries.

In Herberton, seeing such a village again sparked the idea that there should be more of this kind of open-air learning facility. Now with the current influx of so many people from other parts of the world, something clicked. He was able to envisage something really special.

He wanted to help build a shantytown, the only one of its kind in the world, with literally hundreds of examples of the dwellings and shops that people in the third world lived and worked in. He wanted it to be a spectacular educational open-air museum more than anything else, but he felt that it could be a fantastic drawcard for tourists as well. If the job was done properly, it would be a real eye-opener. Alex felt he knew exactly how such a village could work.

He'd always known that there was something lacking in people's understanding of life in the developing world—lord knows in his travels he met some ignorant people. Opening the eyes and minds of these people to methods by which others were forced to live outside developed countries could only have a positive effect. In recent years he'd worried about the growing racist attitudes worldwide and was embarrassed by the treatment that many asylum seekers received. He felt that the problem of racism too could be helped with his shantytown idea. He didn't feel he was being naïve, but any method through which people could experience what life was like for others who struggled to make ends meet or in some instances, just to stay alive, was bound to be positive. Fiona supported him at every turn and helped with every hurdle.

In this unusual and unique village, Alex envisaged sections representing all continents. There'd be an African section, a South American section, an Asian section, an Oceanian section and more—whatever the refugees, in consultation with the necessary planning authorities and a committee that would be formed, thought best. Houses, lean-tos, shops, stores and even markets typical of these regions could be on display with handicrafts and products likely to be found in these parts of the world, available for sale. Most importantly though, the vast majority of people involved in building the town and then afterwards, in staffing the place would be either refugees or migrants who had recently been welcomed to Australia.

After his first letter was published, several websites took up the cause, and one of the major current affairs programs ran a story on his ideas. People all over social media immediately began to chat and many came up with additional suggestions, regarding both the farm assistance plan and also the more exciting Shantytown plan. A few open-minded politicians encouraged farmers to come forward as potential recipients of a refugee family and the plan was set in motion. The federal member for the northern rivers of New South Wales was most excited and came on board encouraging a well-known and iconic Australian entrepreneur to be a part of the Shantytown plan and within a few months a 75 hectare property had been purchased north of Byron Bay and inland a bit, accessible from a new stretch of the improved Pacific Highway, perfectly suitable for a development such as this one which soon passed the planning stage and was ready to begin.

It was an exciting period in the lives of many people. Alex was excited that both his dreams were coming true. A friend whose job was in publicity suggested he pull back a bit and not do all the interviews he was asked to do. This was very good advice. Within a few short weeks of his letters being published, dozens of refugee families had started work on farms throughout the country and within a few months, the idea, like Alex predicted, went ahead in leaps and bounds.

And regarding the building of Shantytown, for many of those

involved in the lead-up to the turning of the first sod including the refugees, its construction became the most exciting event in their lives. There'd been such a general lack of empathy for many of the refugees who, through no fault of their own, had to flee their homeland, sometimes enduring months or even years of absolute hardship. Now, genuinely feeling like they'd been rescued by a nation of warm and welcoming people, they were on the whole ecstatic about their new lives.

The Shantytown idea had developed so quickly. Popular ideas sometimes just flourish. When the first part of Alex's plan was instantaneously so successful and farmers were experiencing the immediate benefits of refugee involvement, part two of his plan simply took off. He'd suggested involving Vietnam War veterans in one of his interviews as he'd come to the realisation that in Australia they'd been pretty neglected over the years. He never became a soldier, but he felt strongly about those who had and the subsequent suffering they were forced to endure. 'Disabled people too might benefit from some form of involvement,' he told the same interviewer.

It wasn't long before over a hundred war veterans, a few of them severely disabled, helped nearly 250 refugees and former refugees and migrants bring the dream to reality in a construction period that took a little over a year, many of the buildings being relatively simple to construct. As well, at the main entrance to the village, they built a few more substantial buildings to house a museum and offices plus a sixty-bed motel, and an amazing restaurant area, a bit like a giant food hall, to demonstrate the cooking styles of the countries represented. There was also a small auditorium and a theatre. These more substantial buildings slowed the project down a bit, but together with the refugee group, the Veterans, a small team of local builders and other tradesmen had the whole village completed in just over the twelve months planned.

Alex had been asked to be on the advisory board of Shantytown to offer ideas right from the beginning and he accepted graciously. Inside, he was thrilled to have been asked and found it exciting to be involved to say the least. Alex wanted to open up a world of knowledge that he felt was missing in the education of children first of all, but also of all members of society in Western cultures. 'Not enough is known about our world,' he said frankly, 'certainly not the developing world. Kids today know about the US, smart phones and gadgets which actually dumb-down the population rather than do what the buyers of all this techno stuff think they do.' And as far as their schooling is concerned, some subjects could actually be replaced with more important life-lessons as he referred to them.

He had always been impressed at how the camp they built in Zambia had evolved, how lessons had changed and developed and felt this should happen everywhere.

When the final jobs were being completed on Shantytown, an impressive village had been created. Fifteen different countries were represented from the continent of Africa, twelve from South & Central America, eleven from Asia, eight from the Middle East and seven from Oceania including an Aboriginal Meriam house of the Torres Strait Islands (twentieth century) and a spinifex shelter typical of the real outback (nineteenth century). Australia, it was decided early in the project, needed to be included simply because some people who live on this continent have not lived, and do not live, a modern sophisticated developed-world existence. To include some examples of Aboriginal dwellings was a very good move.

Because of his time years before in south-east Asia, Alex had taken particular interest in the construction of the thatched-roof Vietnamese home, elevated on wooden poles so as to keep animals out and as protection from the wet ground of Vietnam. Also of interest to him was the Zambian cottage made from mud and grass. However it was the amazing cross-section and differences depicted between the many countries represented that made the village so spectacular.

The official opening saw thousands of excited visitors from all over Australia, an international contingent and hundreds of media representatives arrive to join in on this big event. So many representatives of the press were there.

Built as an educational experience more than anything else, a labyrinth of tracks took visitors from one region to the next with informative signboards for those wanting the traditional explanation of what was what, but also available was the more modern wireless headphone-style of interpretative tour. People who grew up in the styles of houses and lean-tos depicted from all corners of the world were there for visitors to ask questions. Demonstrations ran continually with all sorts of handicrafts being made like carpets and rugs, clothes and knick-knacks. There was a furniture construction area, people doing timber whittling, several blacksmiths, potters, jewellery makers and a large array of fascinating displays could be viewed.

The exotic culinary delights from places like India, Senegal, Paraguay and beyond blew everyone away. The range and quality of the unique foods which were offered from the dozens of countries represented was astonishing. There were literally hundreds of unusual choices of foods and dishes available. And considering that Australia's multi-cultural society had in recent years already provided a fantastic range of foods, what was on offer in Shantytown was almost overwhelming.

What was to excite some people most though was the music. Music from a large number of countries was going to be on show. Alex had secretly harboured ambitions most of his life to somehow involve himself with music. When he and Fiona were in Vietnam this dream came a step closer when he heard the sublime street music of a particular musician they came across in a small out-of-the-way village in the middle of nowhere. Playing the *Dan Bau*, the old man made the single string instrument sing in the most captivating way. Alex was truly mesmerised and hoped that one day he could encourage the movement of such musicians to the West for recitals and the like, for no other reason than to share with the world music that people weren't used to hearing.

It happened often during his travels that he witnessed unusual instruments being played, and the experience was always out of this world.

Now, here in Shantytown, instruments like the West African kora, a 21 string instrument resembling the harp, as well as the djembe, udu and balafon, the pipes and flutes of South America, the drums, ocarina and slit gongs of the Pacific and Oceania, the Vietnamese erhu and danmo, the Indian sitar and literally hundreds of other highly unusual instruments were going to offer spine-tingling sensations for everyone lucky enough to experience them. Alex was ecstatic with every facet of the town, but especially the part that music played in the experience.

And like everywhere throughout Shantytown, each and every person demonstrating the music was to be a refugee or migrant, all keen to impart their knowledge and skills to the Australian public, and of course to international visitors too.

So, the opening day had arrived. The press was filming, dignitaries were in place, speech notes at the ready, and the place was really buzzing. It was the NSW premier who spoke first.

'Ladies and gentlemen, welcome,' he began. 'Welcome to the most unusual theme park in Australia, perhaps the most unusual in the world. What you will be able to meander around shortly is the finest example of its kind anywhere on earth. This was not the dream of an aspiring entrepreneur, nor that of a savvy businessman with a clever plan. Instead it was the idea of a new arrival to our country, someone we've embraced as one of our own. And it wasn't his only idea. Many of you will have heard of the outstanding success that the farming community throughout Australia has experienced by involving refugees to help struggling farmers recently. This too was his idea. And that man, ladies and gentlemen, is this man on my left, Alexander Van der Sluijs.'

The premier began to applaud and everybody else joined in. Alex grinned from ear to ear, although he didn't really like the attention. Fiona was a proud partner side stage.

Continuing on the premier added, 'The Australian farming community is greatly indebted to Alexander's initial idea. For years they'd been doing it tough. Now, things have changed drastically. Not just small towns, but entire communities have been drawn together all helping each other. Innovative businesses have started up as a result. It's nothing short of amazing. And, ladies and gentlemen, I think the same is about to happen here at Shantytown. This is a lot more than examples of dwellings from countries across the globe and it's a lot more than the foods people enjoy in different countries. It's the music, it's the arts and crafts and perhaps most importantly, it's the interaction that we will all have with the people who work here, the very people whose houses, businesses, markets and way of life are on display for us all to learn from. And there is just so much to learn in this wonderful town.'

Speeches are speeches and after the premier finished, the others who followed him waffled on a bit, but when Alex cut the ribbon and the people had the chance to look around, the village was considered unanimously to be a great success.

All sorts of people congratulated Alex in person. Some patted him on the back, shook his hand, others smiled, waved and gave a respectful nod.

The prime minister of Canada, Justin Trudeau dressed so casually and not looking at all like a world leader, pulled Alex aside and said, 'You've helped develop an excellent idea here, Mr Van der Sluijs. I love this place.' He was sporting a big grin as he asked, 'Would you like to come to Canada and help build another one of these fine villages?'

Alex was shocked but overjoyed. 'Of course I'd love to. It would be an honour.'

And so a couple of months later Alex and Fiona were on a plane to Vancouver about to embark on a new journey, yes, another one. Would anyone be surprised? Alex was going to help build a version of his idea that incorporated a lot more than he ever dreamed of. Double the size of the Australian Shantytown, this new village was to be constructed in two distinct sections, one specifically depicting Canadian and Inuit buildings, and the other depicting buildings from the rest of the world.

Trudeau had been impressed with the number of disabled folk who had been involved in the Australian Shantytown and directed his team to invite interested people from all of Canada's disabled groups to get involved in whatever capacity they felt they could. Of particular concern to the prime minister was the alarming rate of attempted suicides in indigenous communities like Attawapiskat in northern Ontario, and so people from this community were invited to be involved too, specifically designing and constructing a home typical of that region. It offered Attawapiskat and similar communities an opportunity to be involved in a very rewarding project.

So even before Alex arrived, people were being interviewed from indigenous communities like this and from all walks of life and all levels of disability hoping to be part of the design, building and eventual running of the village. At first, mixing people who have disabilities with refugees was considered a potential volatile mix, but those chosen were done so with such great care and compassion that the eventual combination of workers was ideal.

There were administrative and clerical jobs on offer, design and construction positions, sales and marketing appointments and a lot more. People were being interviewed for jobs eighteen months in advance of the positions being needed, as it was considered that this village would take about a year and a half to construct. Unlike the Australian version, the Canadian Shantytown was to have a much larger accommodation area. People would be able to stay overnight in a quaint but extremely comfortable hotel as well as a large variety of the actual cottages depicted throughout the village. There was also to be a natural history museum and a campus of the University of British Columbia.

Throughout the construction of the village, many on the board considered that the original name Vancouver Shantytown Village was somewhat of a misnomer as the complex spread impressively over 120 hectares and was to have no fewer than 300 buildings. It was decided therefore to drop the word 'village' and simply call the place Vancouver Shantytown.

It was fast becoming so much more impressive than the original Australian version, but Alex was receiving weekly reports from Australia and he was chuffed at the figures. Thousands were coming through the gates each week, with a steady increase in both day visitors and those staying overnight, including school groups. Of great interest though was the fact that politicians and business leaders from abroad were visiting, most likely with the thought of doing something similar in their own countries.

This Shantytown was different, no doubt about it. Whereas the Australian Shantytown had individual examples of the homes, shops and markets of the third world, the Canadian version in some sections was to incorporate entire villages, clusters of dwellings, and as well, perhaps surprisingly, a replica of a bombed out Beirut city block, plus a number of audio visual displays from other war zones. This Shantytown was therefore considerably different to the original one in Australia. And for visitors to get around this unusual town, rickshaw rides were offered. However, so as not to detract from the authenticity of the displays, they had to keep to the main trails only, just like the bicycles. Other than that it was foot traffic only, and wheelchairs of course.

Completion date was nearing and the final touches were being added to the roads and bike trails. Solar panels by the hundred had been installed on the larger, more contemporary and substantial buildings, and even a few dozen wind generators had been positioned on the hill adjoining the property. No longer referred to as a village it was hardly even a town anymore. It was a mini-metropolis, and soon it would be providing all its own power needs and employing over a thousand people. As well, a large proportion of the fresh produce required in the many restaurants and food stalls was to be grown on site in greenhouses. Seedlings had been propagated out-of-season so as to maximise growth of an abundance of fruits, vegetables and herbs almost year-round and, considering the problems of frost and sub zero temperatures, these greenhouses were state-of-the-art food production centres.

Alex quietly admitted that this was a far cry from what he first envisaged with the initial Shantytown back in Australia, but Prime Minister Trudeau and his team of advisors started pushing right from the beginning to make this a spectacularly modern and impressive example of self-sufficiency as well as a town full of the homes, shops and markets of the developing world. It was a strange marriage of ideas, but one which was poised to work well and to turn heads.

'We don't want to be the isolationist world that America is. They're seriously still considering building that wall in the south along the border with Mexico. We instead want to open our minds and actually learn something from the developing world,' one journalist wrote as the town neared completion.

When the gates opened for the first time in the summer of 2018, that's exactly what started happening. People began to understand in a better sense what life was like in the developing world, what struggles people had to deal with on a daily basis, how difficult it was for some just to stay alive.

By the end of the same year, two other shantytowns were under construction, one on the border of Germany and the Netherlands in a collaborative effort by both governments, and another in Austria, which was to be an inside museum, an EFTE construction in three giant stadiums. The number employed during and after construction in the five shantytowns exceeded twenty thousand. The number of people enlightened by the shantytown experience was far, far greater.

Alexander had certainly achieved something monumental.

And now you the reader have heard my story. It was longer than I said it would be at the beginning when I sat you down. And I have an admission to make about being a friend of Alexander. I am not just any friend. I am the friend who Alexander met when we were in our twenties and lived for a while on the island of Paros. I am the friend who said 'no' to his continual suggestions of travel, of joining him on his voyage of discovery, just so that I could return to the conservative country of my birth, Germany, and study music. I am Barbara. I did study music then taught it all my life, and it has been a good and at times an interesting life. But not as it could have been, had I said 'yes' to Alexander instead of 'no'. That would have changed things as you can imagine, certainly for the love of his life, Fiona, whom he may never have met.

I searched for years on and off trying to find him. It was quite depressing for me. I knew within days of farewelling him that I'd made the wrong decision. Nine months later, back in Munich in the heart of Bavaria, on a cold and wintry morning, I gave birth to his child. I called him Alex. He was a wonderful boy and now is a very good doctor. He is a surgeon and works in Africa for the group Médecins Sans Frontières saving lives. Alexander would have been proud to know his son as he grew up. He was always searching for answers to everything, excelling at school both scholastically and at sport. He is loved by all who encounter his warm and respectful manner, his wicked sense of humour and his skilled surgical hands.

Alex's father is no longer with us. I never found him, even though I visited Paros several times over the years. I suppose we may have crossed paths even more often, as his travels were more extensive than any person I've ever had the pleasure of knowing. When Alex first found out details of my research into his father's life, he referred to him as the modern day Marco Polo.

It was strange how I discovered details about his life. By chance, I picked up a magazine in which there was a story about the Vancouver Shantytown. I wrote to the journalist and he put me in touch with Fiona. She invited me to Paros where she still lives and where Alexander had not long passed away. They came back here permanently after the Vancouver Shantytown was finished. That same year Fiona's mother died and there seemed no need to return to the southern hemisphere anymore. They both lived on Paros for the final years of Alexander's life, going nowhere. He'd finally found a musical instrument that appealed to him, one given to him by a farmer from Kashmir, the sarinda, but his favourite was always the bouzouki. He played the instrument accompanied by Fiona on her flute, they lovingly looked after their garden and he painted most days right up until he died.

Fiona welcomed me into their home and showed me his extensive collection of art from around the world, and his own major works too that he had kept. She showed me their first home, preserved more or less how it was when they lived in it all those years ago. Their two houses though have now been encroached by others; such is the development of twenty-first century life almost everywhere. Fiona invited me to stay, to read his diaries and hers, to delve through newspaper clippings and photo albums of their life. Amongst his drawings I found sketches of myself that he'd drawn fifty years earlier. This brought tears to my eyes naturally.

It was Fiona's kindness and generosity that encouraged me to write their story. I took up residence in the first of their homes looking over the little corner of the Mediterranean which is theirs and now after a summer of writing I have finished their story.

I hope you the reader have enjoyed the journey. I most certainly have.

Moon over the Mediterranean
G J Maher

ISBN: 9781925367898	Qty	.....
RRP	AU$24.99	.....
Postage within Australia	AU$5.00	.....

TOTAL* $_____

* All prices include GST

Name: ....

Address: ....

....

Phone: ....

Email: ....

Payment: [ ] Money Order   [ ] Cheque   [ ] MasterCard   [ ]Visa

Cardholder's Name:...

Credit Card Number: ....

Signature:..

Expiry Date: ....

Allow 7 days for delivery.

Payment to: Marzocco Consultancy (ABN 14 067 257 390)
PO Box 12544
A'Beckett Street, Melbourne, 8006
Victoria, Australia
admin@brolgapublishing.com.au

BE PUBLISHED

Publish through a successful publisher.
Brolga Publishing is represented through:
• **National** book trade distribution, including sales, marketing & distribution through Dennis Jones and Associates Australia.
• **International** book trade distribution to
 • The United Kingdom
 • North America
 • Sales representation in South East Asia
• **Worldwide e-Book distribution**

For details and inquiries, contact:
Brolga Publishing Pty Ltd
PO Box 12544
A'Beckett St VIC 8006

Phone: 0414 608 494
markzocchi@brolgapublishing.com.au
ABN: 46 063 962 443
(Email for a catalogue request)